LIMANG ARAW SA PALAWAN

LIMANG ARAW SA PALAWAN

ZARA IRIGO

Zara Irigo Publishing

First Printing, 2017

FOR IDA

Contents

I

Five Days

"Excuse me," she called for a waiter.

Luck? I was never really a believer in the stuff. Shit happened. We made our own fate. Things happened for a reason. Whatever. Whether it was a coincidence, an unfortunate circumstance, or just plain dumb luck—I'd just gotten back from the city that day and just so happened to be passing by the resort's dining area at that exact moment.

"Yes, ma'am?" I asked.

"Isang mineral water," she requested.

"Mineral water po?" I repeated for confirmation, then went over to the bar to place the order.

I worked all around at our resort: management, maintenance, driver, porter, waiter. But then the resort always prided itself in its excellent service. As I waited, I tapped my fingers on the bar and surveyed the scene.

Our resort was located in the small town of Napsan, fifty-seven kilometers from Puerto Princesa City proper. Our tag line was "Experience nature" because the resort was so tucked away at the edge of the island, practically in the middle of nowhere. It was considered an event to go down to the city. For instance, I had to go earlier today to haul the food supply up to the resort since my dad was already at our restaurant in the city, busy with guests. But the resort had its perks. It was quiet and beautiful. The perfect location for the ultimate summer getaway.

The resort was only half full today. The girl had come with the bunch of people that the resort drivers had picked up from the airport this morning. I figured she was with some tour group, maybe the Japanese ones or the Germans who were walk-ins, but she ate alone. She was probably waiting for some other people. I remembered I'd had her bags brought up to Cottage #3, a room for two with optional extra bed. Not that it mattered either way. I hardly bothered myself with the private businesses of the guests.

"Mineral water po, ma'am." I delivered the bottle to her table.

"Thank you," she said.

I was starting to walk away when she called my attention again. "Uh, excuse me."

I stopped and turned to look, my eyebrows raised expectantly. "Po?"

"Ilang taon ka na?" she asked.

"Uh, twenty-two," I replied, rethinking the "po" since she looked no older than I was. But her next question blew me away.

"May girlfriend ka na?"

"Ha?" I thought I heard her wrong. It wasn't like nobody had ever asked me that question before. It just wasn't a question anyone would normally ask a complete stranger.

She didn't even flinch. "May girlfriend ka na ba?" she repeated.

"Um, wala," I replied, narrowing my eyes at her, trying to guess where she was going with this.

"Gusto mo magkaroon?" she asked.

I must've looked at her funny because she amended instantly. "For five days lang." She raised her hand—five fingers.

"Huh?" I furrowed my eyebrows, looking at her like she was crazy.

"Five days lang," she repeated with a shrug. "Tapos, tapos na."

It was the strangest request I'd ever heard from a guest and I'd encountered quite a few strange ones myself: hypoallergenic pillows, an intercom service, or like. . . dry cleaning. And she made it sound like it was nothing, like she was deciding dine-in or take-out, instead of a supposed commitment.

She must've finally noticed my mystified reaction that she laughed and I realized she must've just been kidding. I blew out a breath in relief. But then she continued with the same unflinching resolved expression.

"Hindi nga. Game?" she prompted. "As in seryosong

boyfriend ha?" she explained patiently. "'Yung tipong kunwari three months na tayo."

"Huh?" I raised my eyebrows at her definite specifications. "Para saan?" I asked warily. *Dare? Drama class? Experiment?* I tried to guess. I didn't know why I didn't just tag her as mentally unstable and walk away. But as the saying went, curiosity usually did kill the cat.

"Wala lang," she replied nonchalantly. "Trip."

"Uhh . . ."

She gestured for me to sit down. "Dali na, five days lang," she urged. "After that, you can just pretend na walang nangyari. We don't have to keep in touch or be friends or anything. You can pretend you didn't meet me at all. Walang catch, promise." She raised her right hand.

I watched her cautiously. She looked nothing but serious. I looked around furtively to see if maybe she was with some people who were just watching for my reaction or anything, like those gag shows on TV.

"Come on, what have you got to lose?" she coaxed. "You don't have to introduce me to your family or anything. You don't even have to buy me presents or have anniversaries or anything stupid like that. Pero siyempre you have to like, you know, act like a boyfriend and everything." She shrugged like it was as simple as snapping your fingers, which by the way I didn't actually find to be that simple.

"Five days?" I repeated vaguely, wondering myself why I was even considering it.

She nodded. "Yeah, five days lang naman ako dito eh," she

told me. "After that—" She waved her hand. "Zip, zilch. Like nothing. Promise. Ano?" she prompted.

"Boyfriend . . ." The mere sound of the word made me cringe as I remembered several distinct instances in the past and a truckload of reasons that reminded me exactly why I currently didn't have a girlfriend, such as it was such a hassle and that I didn't have time for it right now. "Tipong dapat lagi tayo magkasama?" My eyebrows furrowed.

"'Di naman lagi," she replied.

"Tipong nag-de-date, ganun?" I wanted to know.

"Minsan."

She probably recognized the appalled expression on my face when it occurred to me that I was close to flat broke and she let out another slight laugh. "Don't worry about the money." She shrugged again. "Ano, game ha? Five days lang." She put her hand out to shake mine to seal the deal.

I looked at her hand contemplatively, trying to guess how serious she might actually be about the whole thing. For all I knew, she could be asking the question just to see how people would react to such a crazy offer. I looked back up at her. There was no hidden tweak in her smile, no hint of humor. I was slightly intrigued.

Five days. It didn't seem that long a period of time. Anyway, what was the worst that could happen? It wasn't like I was really going to take her seriously. As far as I was concerned, she could do anything she wanted. If she wanted to think she was the first woman on the moon, for example, I wasn't going to stop her.

Besides, if agreeing to anything would get her to shut up and let me leave, I'd agree twice. I pursed my lips in contemplation and hesitated for two seconds before I reached over and shook her hand briefly.

She stopped short, my hand trapped in hers.

I met her gaze.

"Seryoso ako ha?" she started solemnly. "Since agree ka na, request ko lang, please 'wag mong i-treat as a joke, okay? Five days lang, solid, bawal back-out."

"Bawal back-out?" I raised an eyebrow suspiciously.

She rolled her eyes before she released my hand. "No strings attached. Walang catch. Kung gusto mo, awayin mo pa ako for the next five days, basta boyfriend kita, okay?"

I blinked and nodded. "Okay . . ."

"Great!" she smiled brightly and instantly changed moods, changed personalities even, as she reached for my hand across the table again. "Gutom ka ba? You want to order?" she asked. "Here, I still have some crispy pata left. Masarap siya ha," she commented. "Actually, ang sarap lahat ng food n'yo, especially 'yung chopsuey. You want some?"

She was *so* strange. "Uh, teka, may kailangan pa 'kong gawin, eh." I stood to leave, only then able to extricate my hand from her death trap, sort of unsure how to make an exit from a supposed "girlfriend."

"Ah okay." She just continued to eat. "Ay." She looked up. "Ano nga pala name mo?" she asked, as if an afterthought.

I winced. *Oo nga pala.* "Um, Chris," I answered.

She narrowed her eyes at me. "Chris for Christian or Christopher?" she prompted.

I wondered how it mattered. "Christopher," I replied anyway.

She nodded, smiling. "Topher," she said, giving me a new name. "'Yun na itatawag ko sa 'yo," she declared.

I furrowed my eyebrows. "Eh kung Christian pala pangalan ko?" I asked, curiously.

She replied as if it was so obvious. "Ian."

I wanted to roll my eyes at her absurdity but decided it didn't matter to me and I had better things to do. I started to walk away. I was already out the door and halfway to the cottages when I stopped in mid-stride, remembering that I'd forgotten to ask for *her* name.

After a slight pause, I continued walking. I had five days to find out her name. Not that I actually needed to know. Besides, if she was *that* impulsive, she'd probably forget about the whole crazy deal in the next twenty minutes, right?

2

The Prize

I jumped in surprise when just two hours later, I was seated with a few of the staff, having an informal meeting at one of the beach front huts, and she suddenly popped up beside me, looping her arm around mine automatically.

"Hi," she greeted me with a big smile.

I blinked, not quite sure what to make of the situation. "Uh, hi," I said, freezing where I stood.

"Swimming lang ako ha?" she said before she walked away headed to the beach.

Arnold, one of the senior staff and sort of my dad's personal assistant shot me a strange look. "Sino 'yun?" he asked, craning his neck to see where she went, as did everyone else.

"Naku, nakabingwit ka na naman ba, Kristoper?" Mang Sario, the groundskeeper—butchering the pronunciation of my name—asked me with a mischievous smile on his already wrinkled face.

"Oo nga, naalala pa namin si Sssandra," Joseph, one of the cooks, teased, referring to a foreign guest we had last year with whom I had a short encounter. Note: *She* had come on to *me* then left a week later. It was hardly anything.

"Ano nga ba 'yun? Gesunday?" Arnold asked, mispronouncing the German word for health "*Gesundheit.*"

"Gesunday!" Mang Sario cheered.

"Ang kulit n'yo. Tumigil nga kayo." I had to roll my eyes, shaking my head in ridicule.

"Oy, at least Pilipina naman ngayon," Joseph commented. "Mas magkakaintindihan kayo."

Hah! Asa pa! She may have been a local, but she sure seemed like she was from a different planet.

"So, ano na nga, Chris?" Arnold nudged me suggestively. "Naka-iskor ka ba?"

"Naku, mapapagalitan ka na naman ng tatay mo!" Joseph warned.

I made a face, slightly miffed. "Hindi ko kaanu-ano 'yun," I declared firmly. "Isa sa mga guests lang 'yun," I answered. "Medyo may sayad 'ata."

The last thing I needed was for these guys to tease me about a psycho pseudo-girlfriend. I didn't care to deny her since a) technically it wasn't really true, b) she wouldn't find out anyway, and c) they were really starting to annoy me.

"Tama na nga 'yan," I dismissed irritably. "May pag-uusapan pa tayo," I started with my authoritative I'm-the-boss tone, which fortunately still worked, unlike my brain which obviously ceased to function the moment I decided to shake her hand.

***

Her name was Mia. She didn't give me a hard time about it, or gotten mad that I only then asked, which I guessed didn't really matter.

I watched her strangely as she sat across from me under a beach hut. The rest of the staff had left after the meeting when she cornered me, coming back from the beach. She'd initially asked me to go swimming with her but I'd refused, saying I hadn't brought a swimsuit—which was of course just a sneaky lie—so she just settled to talking incessantly about anything and apparently everything that passed through her flighty head for the next thirty minutes. But I didn't want to be rude. I was going to draw the line at forty-five minutes, at most an hour.

I vaguely heard something about her sister who was supposed to have come with her to the resort but got held up at work so would be coming later in the week or something. She talked briefly about sunburns, beach insects, other resorts, how strange it was that ours didn't have keys for the cottages. She talked about Palawan—dusty roads, legends she heard about Puerto Princesa, etc.

She didn't care that I didn't contribute anything to the conversation, didn't care that I didn't talk at all. I didn't think she even cared to know if I was really listening. I was just nodding my head every so often, thinking of the quickest, most plausible way to extricate myself from her company and starting to stress myself out about it as time wore on that I couldn't think of one.

I took out a stick from the pack of cigarettes in my pocket and tapped the filter on my palm as usual.

"Ah! You smoke!" she exclaimed, aghast.

I stopped from raising the cigarette to my mouth and looked over. "Bakit?"

She made a face. "I don't kiss smokers," she said and I almost choked on my own spit.

I shot her a weird look. "Um, alam mo, okay lang talaga," I resigned, lighting the stick and taking a puff. I didn't care if she stayed far away from me for the next five days. And I wasn't expecting perks of *any* kind. It wasn't that she was repulsive or anything. To be honest, she had her finer points and I normally wouldn't pass up such an opportunity, but I just really didn't feel like being "obligated" to. I hardly knew her. I doubted if I could possibly be able to get to know her enough within just the five days. Plus, she was kinda nuts.

I took a drag again and puffed out smoke.

"Ay, may gagawin pa pala ako. Sige." She stood up just like that and walked away.

I blinked surprised. What the—? I watched her disappear past the hedges headed back to the beach and just shook my head to myself in disbelief. *Baliw.*

3

Girlfriend

She was more than mentally unstable. She was manic-depressive. She was incredibly moody. She was probably even borderline schizophrenic. She'd be gone for hours then pop up later and pester me with requests and stories and jokes. And she certainly had no reservations with regards to touch as she felt free to hold my hand, touch my hair, put my arm around her shoulders—things real couples did. Granted, she was amusing to a point but her abundant enthusiasm got tiring, not to mention exceedingly annoying as time wore on. And it had only been a day. I was fast becoming a punch line for jokes among the staff, which frankly I needed as much as a gastric ulcer. Like the guys didn't have enough to tease me about.

Sprawled on one of the rattan sofas we had in the living area, I was trying to watch the Lakers vs. Blazers game on satellite cable when she walked in and unceremoniously sat right next to me. I stared at her strangely. She didn't say anything, her eyes glued to the TV. I turned back to the TV slowly, warily, as if expecting her to pounce any moment.

She moved suddenly to reach for the ashtray and put out my cigarette.

"Oy!" I protested, frowning—too late. That was the third time today that she'd either taken my cigarette from me or had put it out without asking for my permission. I threw up my hands helplessly in exasperation, knowing it was pointless to argue. I settled to frowning as I turned back to the game.

"Ano 'yan?" she asked, referring to the TV, as if she'd done nothing that just recently upset me.

"Basketball," I replied shortly as the game went into double overtime.

She fidgeted in the seat next to me, and kept fidgeting, disturbing me in the process.

I was just trying to get some peace and quiet after a long day. I wanted to watch TV—alone. Apparently, that didn't happen when you had a girlfriend. She was starting to irritate me—again. "Pwedeng 'wag kang malikot?" I asked, edgily, when the game went into a timeout.

She blinked at me surprised then pouted, the way "girlfriends" do 'pag nagtatampo.

I didn't care. I ignored her. This was my resort. I'd do what I want. I watched the game again.

She shifted on the seat again, sideways so she leaned back on the armrest, her feet propped on my lap.

I glanced at her slightly but didn't move. She was watching TV again, her eyebrows furrowed as if she were really concentrating on the game. I guessed she was going to shut up now. Good.

During a commercial break, she fidgeted again, shifting on the seat closer beside me but didn't say anything. She just tilted her head and stared at my face. I shot her a questioning look but since she wasn't doing anything to disturb me, I didn't say anything. When the game started again, she reached up to touch my face.

I wove away automatically. "Ano'ng ginagawa mo?"

She just blinked up at me innocently. "Wala."

I shot her a strange look—just briefly because I was still trying to concentrate on the game. I thought if I ignored her maybe she'd quit it. Besides, O'Neal was fouled out and the Blazers were in the lead—104-102.

But then she started to play with my ears. I tried to move my head away in irritation. "Oo na, malaki na," I grumbled, not taking my eyes off the TV, as I was used to being teased about my ears all my life. They weren't my fault. They were my dad's genes.

"No, I like it," she commented. "It's cute."

"'Wag," I tried to shrug her off. Didn't work. She traced my cheekbones. "I like all the parts of your face," she said loudly. I guessed it was supposed to be some kind of twisted compliment but I really wasn't in the mood for her antics.

Darius Miles bumped into Derek Fisher, fouling on a loose ball. I craned my neck to see the TV past her head. Her knees were now propped on my lap so I couldn't move away to see better. Aggravated, I furrowed my eyebrows. With less than a second left on the clock, Kobe Bryant was attempting a crazy three-point shot from at least twenty-five feet out. The buzzer sounded—just as Mia fidgeted on the seat, her head blocking my view. I missed the basket!

I jumped up in my seat to see the screen, knocking her to one side in the process, and saw that the Lakers had won 105-104, therefore making the playoffs and making the Blazers miss it for the first time in like twenty seasons. "Aaaaahh," I groaned loudly in frustration glared at her. "Ano ka ba? Wala ka bang ibang maistorbo?" I demanded with a threatening tone.

She looked back at me for a moment, surprised then folded her arms over her chest stubbornly. "Sinong tinakot mo?"

I glared at her in exasperation before I roughly stood up and walked out of the living area.

One day down. Four to go.

4

Quarantine

I'd developed a hawk's eye where she was concerned in the past thirty-six hours, knowing her exact location at any given time so I could be ready to avoid her at all costs.

Today she was seated alone at one of the beach huts on the garden area, reading her cellphone. She seemed to be highly concentrated on what she was texting, her eyebrows furrowed and her expression kept changing like she was mulling over something in her head.

She'd come up to me earlier in the day, as cheerful as usual, probably not caring that I was a little more than slightly miffed at her from last night, and chattered for a few minutes, like nothing was wrong, before she went on her way back to the beach to go swimming again, which was *all* she did apparently. She'd already gotten a hard tan.

In the afternoon, I had been lounging on one of the chairs out on the beach, trying to relax. I closed my eyes for one second, and the next thing I knew, she'd crept up beside me on the chair, settling her head on my shoulder. I gawked at her, but she was asleep before I could say narcolepsy. I'd debated for two minutes whether or not to leave then thought she was already asleep anyway. I shrugged her off and stood up, heading for somewhere else where I could relax and be *alone*.

I was hunched over the bar, reading the newspaper, keeping one eye on her.

Arnold slid into the seat next to me. "Pare, musta syota mo?" he asked teasing.

Mia stood up from her seat, looking left and right as if not knowing where to go or as if looking for something.

I rolled my eyes. I'd already explained to Arnold this morning the unorthodox situation I was currently in and he just laughed at me. I'd told him not to tell the others but in a place as small as this, it was unlikely that they wouldn't find out anyway. "Hindi ko kaanu-ano 'yun," I replied with conviction.

Mia sat back down again, her forehead creasing deeper. She frowned over her cellphone.

Arnold laughed. "Eh ba't panay ang bantay mo?" he asked, patting my back. "Nag-aalala ka baka may ibang makabing-wit?" he asked, kidding around.

"Hay naku," I let out a groan. *Kung pwede nga lang . . .*

"Bakit, mestisa naman a." He elbowed me suggestively. "Saka mukha namang mabait."

"May sayad 'yun," I informed him.

He laughed again. "Huu, 'kaw, takot ka lang yatang magka-sundo kayo eh," he joked. "'Pag ikaw talaga, makakita ng katapat mo, nakow!" he exclaimed.

I rolled my eyes again. "Eh, ewan ko sa 'yo." I stood up and walked towards the beach area to see if maybe some of the guests needed any assistance. I passed the garden area where she was. She looked up when I walked by and seemed to hesitate for about a split second before she called my attention.

I stopped, eyeing her warily. *Now what?*

She smiled brightly as she came up to me and hooked her arm around mine again. "May lakad ka ba later?" she asked. "Pwedeng samahan mo ako sa bayan? May imi-meet kasi akong friends eh," she requested sweetly as if she knew a plain request would get her nowhere, which was correct.

The city was an hour and a half drive away on extremely rough road, two if you didn't know the area, four if your vehicle sucked.

"Pleeeeeease." She wrinkled her nose, in a manner I guessed she thought looked cute.

I hesitated, then hesitated again, then shook my head before sighing in resignation. "Anong oras?" I asked.

Her eyes lit up considerably. "Yey! Alis tayo mga five, okay lang?"

I just shrugged, nodding okay, then kept walking. I normally chauffeured guests to and from the city anyway. Besides, there wasn't any other way out there except if someone drove.

***

"Em!" someone hollered as soon as we stepped into the restaurant. I looked over at the someone who was waving frantically at us. Mia saw them as well and pulled me to head for their table.

Ka Lui's was a popular local restaurant on the Puerto Princesa main road that specialized in seafood so it was usually full at this time of night. Mia's friends had gotten the table on the floor where people sat cross-legged Japanese style. Three girls and three guys. We walked over.

"Hey, guys," Mia greeted.

"Uy, Em! Grabe, ang itim mo na kaagad a!" one girl commented, not even noticing me.

"Naku hassle, di na 'ko pwedeng umitim pa," another chimed in making a face, not noticing me either.

The third girl did though and noted Mia's hand in mine, which by the way wasn't my idea, and looked up at me.

Mia noticed where she was looking at instantly. "'Nga pala, guys," she started without any further ado, "this is Topher." She gestured to me.

A chorus of greetings began directed at me before Mia finished her sentence.

"Boyfriend ko," she said and I hid a cringe. Yes, she said it.

"Haha! Hindi nga!" one guy couldn't help himself.

Mia shot him a look. "Hindi nga," she said seriously.

After an uncertain pause, like he was trying to see if she was really, *really* serious, "Ngee." The guy made a face and met my gaze. "Hehe, sori, tsong. Joke lang. Nice to meet you, pare."

Mia rolled her eyes. "That's Ken," she said to me, then introduced the rest of the people. The three girls were Val, Liezel, and Meenah. The other two guys were Gino and George. George was apparently Liezel's boyfriend.

"Hi." I waved shortly at everyone, feeling uncomfortable and out of place from being the guy nobody else knew, aside from the fact that I had just been introduced as someone's fake boyfriend.

"Nag-order na kami ng food, Em," Val started. "Dagdag na lang kayo."

Mia handed me the menu. "What do you want?"

"Bahala ka na," I said carelessly.

"Sure?" she prompted. "Ako magbabayad," she coaxed with a catch in her voice.

That made me laugh. "Hindi, okay lang, sige, bahala ka na," I replied.

"Huuy, Em," Liezel started. "Ikaw talaga, kahit kelan nang-iiwan ka. Kung 'di ka pa talaga tinext ni Meenah, 'di namin malalaman andito ka rin pala sa Palawan."

Mia made a face at her. "Ngek, 'di n'yo naman ako inimbita in the first place eh may plano pala kayo magbakasyon."

"Teka, teka," the guy named Gino started. "I think we're forgetting a very important issue here," he spoke with a slight Canadian accent. "Em, you never told us you had a boyfriend na ulit ha," he said with a grin.

My eyebrow rose at "ulit" and I listened attentively.

"Oo nga 'no," Val mused out loud. "Wala nga kaming

naririnig na bagong nanliligaw sa 'yo, ngayon may boyfriend ka na kaagad."

Mia smiled sheepishly. "Ehhh, recent lang naman 'to eh," she explained.

"Teka nga, ano ba kayo?" Liezel shushed them. "Si Topher kaya ang tanungin natin. You guys are talking about him like he's not here."

"Oo nga naman," Ken said. "Pare, you have earned the respect of our entire I.T. department. Paano mo napasagot si Em? 'Eh ang taas-taas ng standards niyan?"

I laughed a nervous laugh. *Uh . . .what was I supposed to say to that?*

"Hay naku, guys," Mia interjected. "Leave him alone. Baka masindak n'yo pa 'to nang 'di oras. Sa 'kin pa nga lang, sindak na 'to eh."

They laughed.

I felt slightly offended as she was making me out to be some kind of wuss. "Ako? Sindak?" I had to say. "Hindi kaya," I said defensively.

Mia shot me a yeah-right look, surprised I'd spoken.

"Ay, 'wag kang mag-alala diyan." Meenah patted my back. "Sa simula lang nakakasindak 'yang si Em."

"Kasi sa susunod, nangangagat na!" Ken cut in.

They laughed again. So did I. They were a pretty friendly bunch of people, the kind I could see myself being friends with as well. And Mia adeptly fielded the occasional questions about "us" so I didn't have to say much—let alone lie, but they did try to include me in their conversations. Not to mention,

I was actually talking a lot more than George was, but that didn't seem to bother anyone.

"Naku, Topher, alam mo ba 'yan si Em, sobrang moody n'yan," Liezel started. "Minsan 'kala mo nagloloko, 'yun pala seryoso. Pag akala mo naman seryoso, ginagago ka na pala."

"Pero alam mo," Val started, "ako recently ko lang din natutunan pa'no basahin ang moods ni Em. I mean you can read practically everything from her eyes."

I met Mia's gaze.

She shot me a wary look then looked at everyone else. "Kayo ha," she started to them. "Baka masyadong maraming matutunan si Topher sa inyo."

"Oooh, secrets ba, secrets?" Liezel jeered mischievously.

"Basta, pare, sinasamba ka namin, you da man!" Ken started. "'Lam mo ba 'yan si Em, ang daming nagkakandarapa diyan. Kasi naman, maganda na, matalino pa, sira pa ulo." He laughed. "San ka pa?"

"Kaya nga ang hirap makapasa diyan eh," Gino added with a laugh as well.

All this information was very amusing to me but I somehow could not relate the aggressive-psycho-girl-Mia to this *Em* they were talking about, because *this* Em person actually sounded kind of cool. Then again, they also testified to her being moody. I knew *that*. I was living proof *to* that.

Come to think of it, Mia's excessively bubbly demeanor had gone on a sabbatical. She wasn't as irritating as her usual self, how she normally was with me at the resort. It was kind of weird—weird, but good. At a pause when everyone was busy eating or doing something else, I leaned over to Mia.

"Em?" I prompted questioningly.

"Emilia," she replied coolly.

"Ah." I nodded in understanding. That explained the Chris-Topher phenomenon. "Saang resort sila nag-sa-stay?" I asked as the waiter brought our food.

"Sa Casa Linda ata, tas nag-i-island hopping or something," she explained, reaching for the tempura basket.

I watched her strangely as she started to serve the food right onto my plate. "Uh, thank you," I said tentatively. "S-so hanggang kelan sila?"

"Until Friday 'ata," Mia replied. "Sauce?" she offered, gesturing to the tempura sauce.

I blinked at her. "Uh, hindi, okay na, ako na lang, sige, thanks," I said. "So . . . dadaan ba sila sa resort?" I asked again.

She paused, realizing my concern. "Ah, hindi," she answered. "Tonight lang 'to," she assured. "Relax ka lang." She patted my back encouragingly with a teasing smile.

I laughed under my breath as she had read my mind. I'd probably never see these people ever again anyway. I guessed one night wouldn't hurt. *Besides*, I thought as I watched Mia dump another spoonful of adobong kangkong onto my plate. It wasn't like I had a choice.

5

Q & A

Later on, I noticed her shifting restlessly in her seat. "Bakit?"
I asked.

Mia blinked at me then gave me a wan smile. "Uh, wala,
kasi um . . .kelangan ko mag-CR eh . . ." she trailed off.

She didn't want to leave me in the mercy of her friends
and questions I undoubtedly would not be able to answer. But
then again I thought her friends were pretty harmless. In fact,
I wasn't having as terrible a time as I thought I would. It wasn't
like I couldn't handle a few minutes with them without her. I
mean, what was the worst that could happen?

"Hindi, okay lang. Mag-CR ka na," I urged. "Kaya ko 'to."

"Hindi nga?" She raised her eyebrow at me and grinned.
"Sabi mo 'yan ha." She moved to stand. "CR lang ako, guys,"
she announced.

"Ayooos," Ken howled. "Pwede na mag-Q&A," he teased loudly.

I chuckled under my breath, realizing Mia's earlier concern. She knew them well, yes she did.

"Haha." Mia made a face. "Be nice, guys. 'Wag n'yo masyadong takutin." She winked at me before she left.

"Ha ha!" Gino rubbed his hands mischievously. "Wala na si kumander."

"So, Topher," Liezel leaned over wickedly, "anong ayaw mo kay Em?"

"Naman 'to, ayaw kaagad." Meenah nudged her. "Ano muna nagustuhan mo kay Em?"

"Hindi, hindi," Ken waved dismissively. "Start with the dislikes na."

I looked at each of them flustered at the directness of their questions. "Uh . . ." I paused then cleared my throat. I could handle this. *Ayaw? Madami-dami 'yun*, I thought and made a face. Of course I had to be careful not to say anything too bad that might offend them. These *were* her friends. Hm . . . "Masyado siyang makulit . . . .minsan?" I supplied tentatively.

"'Tol." Ken slung an arm around my shoulders and said with a threatening tone. "'Wag mo kaming pinagloloko ha-"

I blinked at him wordlessly as I was surely no match for two guys who just as well may pummel me into the ground. But then Ken continued. "Anong *minsan*?" he asked, dropping the threatening aura for his normal comical one. "Si Em? *Sobrang* kulit kaya n'un!"

"Eh siyempre," Val said dismissively like it was so obvious.

"Oo nga, reyna ng kakulitan 'yan si Em." Liezel nodded in agreement.

I let out a slight laugh in relief. They knew her pretty well too. I was more at ease in continuing. "Saka . . . may pagka-impulsive siya?" I added truthfully. "Parang hindi niya iniisip mga ginagawa niya."

That made them laugh.

"Hay naku, typical Em." Gino shook his head like he already knew this as well.

Ken wagged his finger at me. "Lagot ka, isusumbong ka namin." He laughed a sinister laugh.

"Tama na 'yan," Meenah insisted. "So, ano naman pinakana-gustuhan mo kay Em?" she prompted.

"Siyempre marami," Gino interjected. "*Dapat* marami," he mocked another warning.

"Uh . . ." I broke a sheepish smile and started to think. Hmm . . . *Ano nga ba?* I sorted through the past forty-eight hours in my head. Mia was . . . funny, she was fun to be with, easy to please, malambing, masayahin—that was of course on the times that she didn't annoy me to death. *Pinakagusto?* "Um . . .maalaga siya," I answered with a shrug. "Medyo sweet."

They all stared at me like I'd grown another head.

After a pause, Liezel blinked at me strangely and asked, "Like what do you mean *sweet*?"

"Um . . ." I swallowed. Was that the wrong thing to say? I wondered, but tried to explain. "Um, ano, 'yun bang tipong naiisip niya kung anong kailangan mo tapos ginagawa niya kahit hindi mo naman sinabi. Uh, attentive." An instance struck me. "'Pag kumakain kunwari, siya na naglalagay ng pagkain sa plato ko, saka napapansin niya 'yung mga hindi ko kinakain." This was true which she *had* actually done several times before. Not to mention she actually worried about leaving me behind earlier to go to the bathroom.

"Dudes!" a tall guy walked over to our group with a grin and everyone looked up.

"Langya pare, ang tagal mo a." Ken nodded a greeting up at him.

The guy clasped Gino's hand in greeting before he slumped down beside him and gave us all an apologetic smile. "Sorry, guys, could not be helped."

"Mike, ganda ng timing mo," Val said. "Narinig mo ba 'yun? Si Em daw super sweet."

"Huh?" Mike asked, looking lost.

"Naku, Mike, you missed quite a revelation," Gino started.

"Si Em as in Emilia Garcia?" Mike prompted. "What? Sabi nino?"

"Si Topher pala, pare," Ken told Mike gesturing to me.

"Uy," I greeted shortly, watching him cautiously, wondering what the big deal was.

"Boyfriend ni Em," Gino told him with a catch in his tone I couldn't quite place.

"He says Em's maalaga daw—ang labo!" Liezel laughed a little, making a face.

Bakit? Ano ba si Mia, bato? I felt as though I should defend her. Especially since I didn't understand how they could have missed this plain fact given that they were supposed to be her friends. I frowned. "Hindi nga talaga," I started, "'yun bang 'pag lagi niya pinapatay 'yung yosi ko kasi ayaw niyang naninigarilyo ako." Granted, I initially thought this was rude but it also qualified as thoughtful in any case.

"What? You smoke?" Meenah cut in, in disbelief.

I blinked. *Oops.* "Um, oo." I nodded, warily.

Mia got back just then with a smile. "O ano, napaiyak n'yo ba?" she prompted, teasing, as she slid back into the seat next to me and slipped her hand into mine automatically.

I just shrugged. Everyone else seemed content to shut up.

"Oy, Em, 'kala ko ba I was the last smoker you'd ever go out with?" Mike prompted dryly in an all-knowing, all-conceited, all-authoritative tone of voice—or so it hit me.

No sooner did she hear the voice did her grip on my hand tighten. Her eyes widened for a split second in surprise before she turned, finally seeing him.

"Hoy, Mike, walanghiya ka, nandito ka rin pala," she greeted in a mock sarcastic tone.

I looked at them in turn, unable to ignore the sudden tension in the air.

"Dapat pala dinala ko si Jackie so she can meet your new guy," Mike said airily.

"Ooh," Ken hissed, making a face. "Foul, pare."

Mia didn't miss a beat. "Oo nga pala, there's this conversation I've been putting off that I need to have with her," she said guilelessly.

Ken and Gino both hissed. "Ooh, sapul," Gino commented.

"Hoy hoy, tama na nga kayo diyan," Meenah refereed. "Magorder ka na, Mike. Kayo guys, more drinks?" she prompted everyone else.

Mia ordered another Red Horse.

***

I was only half-listening to Liezel and George tell everyone about their Puerto Galera vacation in two weeks, I could hear Meenah only faintly, and I couldn't hear Mia at all but she looked very disturbed from across the room. I was trying not to eavesdrop, but they had left the table so abruptly plus I didn't have anything else to do anyway. All I could figure was that Mike and Mia probably had some sort of falling out that wasn't too friendly. I instantly resented him.

"Eh kase, if you knew he'd be here, we knew you wouldn't come. It's the past. Tapos na eh," Meenah explained. "Besides, would it have helped if you'd known?"

Mia frowned and said something.

"Handa?" Meenah asked. "Bakit, ano ba ihahanda mo? Balisong? Shotgun?"

Mia just rolled her eyes and said something short before they came back to the table.

This time, probably from all the tension, Mia didn't slip her hand into mine the way she usually did. Strange how you noticed the little things only when they're gone. Her forehead was creased. I debated on whether or not to ask her what was wrong, but then I thought, Mia's problems had nothing to do with me.

After two seconds, Mia sat up in her seat, as cheerful as usual, talking, laughing, making jokes. Even talking to Mike. She seemed back to normal. But I was watching her eyes.

6

Issues

Mia turned on the radio during the ride back, and kept up a minimum level of small talk, commenting on how early people in the province turned in, making fun of her friends, asking me what I thought of Gino's stupid new haircut, explaining to me Ken's iron deficiency that disconnects his brain from his big mouth, and how Liezel was the only one who could get George to start talking. But nothing else. Nothing about earlier. Nothing about her. And I suddenly realized that despite the amount of time that she'd talked in the past two days, she rarely talked about herself.

But I didn't ask. If she didn't want to talk about it, I wasn't going to press. Besides, the last thing I needed was to have to console some chick mooning over some guy that had *nothing* to do with me.

We arrive at the resort at almost midnight. Mia got out of the car. "Thanks pala a." She bade shortly and waved. "Good night," she said and disappeared into the darkness.

I aligned the pickup with the other vans before I hopped out. The resort was all quiet. Everyone had probably turned in already except if Joseph and the guys had decided to have a drinking session on the beach, especially tonight, with the full moon just waning.

I was walking back to the dining cottage to check if any of the other staff might still be awake when I passed Mia's cottage and slowed down, deep in thought.

I didn't know why I was even considering talking to her now, why I thought I should at least check on her. Maybe it was guilt. Yesterday, I'd thought she was just nuts, asking a stranger for a short-term commitment. After tonight, I was guessing there might actually be more to her behavior, like maybe an actual logical explanation.

I just wanted to see if she needed anything, I rationalized. She was a guest anyway.

I took a step toward the cottage then stopped. She must already be sleeping. Or she probably wanted to be alone. OR, I blinked and shook my head clear it. *It was none of my goddamned business*, I told myself sternly, shaking my head in ridicule at my even *having* the idea.

I walked past her cottage zand headed to the dining cottage but all the lights were out. I guessed everyone did turn in early tonight. I started to walk back to my cottage. But on the way, I passed the walkway to the beach and squinted as I thought

I saw something move. I thought it might be Joseph and the guys hanging out on the beach so I headed out there.

The big tree cast shadows on the sand so initially I only made out a figure seated on one of the lounge chairs, facing the water. I was still meters away when I guessed who it was.

Mia didn't look up when I arrived. She was staring straight out into the ocean.

I took the rest of the steps closer tentatively then sat down beside her, since I was already there anyway. I cleared my throat, staring out into the ocean myself before I spoke. "Uy," I mumbled the short greeting.

"Uy," she replied in the same tone, not moving.

I was still thinking of what to say, whether or not to say anything at all. I didn't want to disturb her. She'd probably come out here to be alone and think or something. But I just wanted to make sure she was all right, maybe help her in any way if I could, by maybe just being here.

I heard her take a deep breath, or it could have been a heavy sigh. I glanced over at her. She was still staring out into the night. Instinctively, I moved my hand on the chair and put it over hers. I wanted to let her know she wasn't alone. She didn't respond or move or anything.

Then after about half a minute, I glanced over at her sideways again and my eyes widened in surprise. Mia's eyes were closed, squeezed shut, nothing unusual if I didn't notice tears glistening on her eyelashes. Her lips were pressed tightly together from trying hard not to make a sound and her chin was trembling.

Oh shhh— I sat up alarmed. This wasn't the first time I'd seen a girl cry, of course, but that didn't mean I'd ever learned how to deal with it.

She pulled her hand out from under mine to cover her mouth with both hands as she was starting to breathe in short gasps, her shoulders heaving.

I made a face and raised my hand to pat her back awkwardly, like they did on TV when someone cried, but that only seemed to make it worse. I frowned again, surprised at how much this seemed to affect her. Mike didn't strike me personally as a guy who made much of an impression. Then again, I didn't know anything.

Then she stopped. She stopped crying so suddenly, I wouldn't have known anything was wrong if her cheeks weren't tearstained. She blinked several times, squared her shoulders and cleared her throat, before she stood up and started to walk back towards the resort.

I highly doubted she was anywhere close to done letting it out. "Mia," I called.

"I'm fine," she called dismissively, not stopping.

I watched her walking away, amazed at how strong she was—and stumped and mystified and bewildered and confounded. There weren't enough words to describe it. She was so incredibly insane. Damn . . .

7

It wasn't me

I was walking faster than usual. I'd just come back from the city on another errand for my dad. I was supposed to catch Mia at breakfast because I'd had Joseph make her everything she liked, had the table set up with flowers and everything. I had our lunch and dinner planned too. Unfortunately, I couldn't neglect my managerial responsibilities no matter how much I wanted to.

I still thought she was nuts but I wanted to cheer her up. What could I say? At this resort, we went the extra mile. Anyway, I *was* the supposed "boyfriend." I headed to the dining cottage to see if she was still there, maybe grab a bite myself, try to have an actual two-way conversation with her—already grinning to myself should I be able to accomplish that.

My walking slowed when I didn't see her in the dining

cottage. I frowned as I looked around. Then I noticed a small crowd at the other end of the property, near the river. We were planning to extend the resort to the other side to make way for camping grounds for backpackers. People were coming to survey the land today.

I headed there and spotted Mia, who looked up, met my gaze and waved with a bright smile. I nodded in reply, starting to walk over.

The guy beside her looked up as well and raised his hand to shield his eyes from the sun to see who I was. "Uy, pare," he greeted loudly.

"Uy." I nodded again in reply, squinting in the sun myself. "Leo, kamusta?" I shook his outstretched hand.

Leo used to live in Puerto Princesa and we grew up together part of our lives. He moved to Manila a few years before I did and I came back to Palawan before he did. I saw him around a few times in the city but that's as much interaction as we'd had. He was a typical local, *kayumanggi*, the same height I was, but I most remember him chasing after several different girls at one time—not that he needed to chase them. He was *that* kind of guy. But that didn't mean we weren't still friends.

"Balak n'yo pala gawan 'to ng camping grounds?" Mia asked as she anchored herself to my side, putting her arms around my waist.

I blinked at her but didn't move away. "Uh . . .oo," I replied then looked back up at Leo. "Na-meet mo na pala si Leo," I said instinctively putting my arm around her shoulder.

"Oo naman. Pare, ikaw talaga," Leo told me. "Dapat pala

nadadalas ako ng akyat dito sa inyo, ang gaganda ng mga guests n'yo a." He grinned at Mia, who just laughed.

"Siyempre, world-class kami eh," I said good-naturedly. "Kasama ka pala sa grupo na 'to?" I gestured to the surveyors.

Leo looked up at them. "A oo." He nodded. "Kaka-graduate ko lang kasi ng Engineering sa Manila eh. Balak ko nga mag-take up ng second course eh pero kelangan ko muna kumita." He chuckled.

"Ah." I nodded in understanding. For some weird reason, his story was rubbing me the wrong way, short of arrogant.

"Ows? San ka ba nag-college?" Mia asked, looking interested.

"Sa La Salle," Leo replied with a smile.

"May kapatid akong second year sa La Salle," she told him.

"A talaga?" He nodded. "Ikaw rin 'di ba? Second year high school?" he teased, making fun of her height.

Mia stuck her tongue out at him. "Loko-loko, graduate na rin ako 'no," she said and poked him lightly on the shoulder. "Kanina ka pa a," she said with a warning tone but not looking angry at all.

Leo just laughed.

Kanina pa? My eyebrows furrowed almost involuntarily. Aside from the fact that I'd transferred schools for the past three years so I hadn't exactly graduated in anything and therefore could not relate to their conversation, I didn't like the way Leo was looking at Mia. I nudged her lightly. "Kumain ka na?" I asked.

"Yupyup." She nodded, smiling. "Ang tagal mo eh. Mag-lu-lunch na kaya."

I gave her a sheepish look. "Eh, nautusan ako eh," I explained. "'Lam mo naman ako, dakilang alila lang dito sa resort," I joked.

If Mia was surprised that I was replying in full sentences, unlike how I normally did in our previous conversations, she didn't show it. In fact, she looked just as cheerful as usual that had I not actually seen her last night, I wouldn't have thought this was the same girl. But I wasn't going to ruin her mood and ask her about it now.

"Haha, dakilang alila?" Leo repeated as if in skepticism. "Ikaw? 'Di ba dakilang senyorito ka? Pati nga paghuli ng tuko, inuutos mo pa eh." He was just teasing, but again, it was rubbing me the wrong way.

"Aba, sa pagkakaalala ko, pareho lang tayong takot sa tuko dati ha," I reminded him pointedly.

"Haha oo nga 'no," he said smoothly. "Pero at least ako hindi hanggang ngayon," he joked then nudged me lightly. "Joke lang, pare."

I just rolled my eyes.

"Ang kukulit n'yo," Mia half-groaned and tugged on my shirt. "Lunch na ba? Gutom na'ko."

"Agad?" I asked, taken aback, as I knew how much breakfast I'd had cooked for her.

She pouted. "Ano ba? Masarap eh," she said stubbornly and I couldn't help but laugh. She pulled on my hand, starting to head towards the dining hut. Then before I could say anything, she turned and waved at Leo. "Tara, Leo, kain tayo," she called.

"Ayos," Leo said and, much to my dismay, walked with us

towards the dining cottage, Mia in between us as they continued to "chat."

I mostly just listened. They were talking about college again, about people they knew who might know each other and so and so. I squeezed Mia's hand in mine briefly. "Sa'n ka ba nag-college?" I asked.

"Sa UP," she replied.

"Eh 'yung prof sa ES, 'yung kalbo, ano nga ba pangalan nun?" Leo asked, snapping his fingers in an effort to remember.

"Diaz?" Mia supplied then laughed. "Grabe, ang tamad nun magturo, sobra. Pero ang masaya dun, naka-tres ako sa kanya kahit bano ako sa ES. Pero mabuti na rin, kundi hindi ako naka-graduate on time."

Wow. I couldn't help but be impressed. But I didn't say anything. Leo seemed impressed enough for all of us.

"Wow. Astig," Leo breathed in reverence. "Henyo ka pala," he teased.

"Nyah!" Mia made a face. "Hindi 'no," she said with a little laugh.

It was a little early for lunch so the dining cottage wasn't too crowded yet. We headed towards a table that seated four and I let them sit down. "Sabihan ko lang si Joseph," I said, starting for the kitchen.

"Naks, senyorito talaga," Leo joked.

I rolled my eyes again and just let it slide. *Speak softly and* . . . I headed into the kitchen trying to remember if Leo was allergic to anything. "Joseph," I called, looking around.

"Uy, boss." Tony, another kitchen hand, looked up from the table. "Wala si Joseph. Kasama ata nila boss Arnold."

"Ah okay." I nodded. "Nabilin ba sa 'yo 'yung lunch namin? Chopsuey, crispy pata—" I rattled off.

"A oo." Tony nodded. "Ipapadala ko na lang."

I could hear Mia and Leo laughing from outside the kitchen.

"Hindi, okay lang, ako na." I volunteered, coming over to the table and tried to identify which dishes I was going to bring out as he pointed them out to me.

"Naubos pala 'yung kangkong kaninang umaga," Tony informed me. "Kukuha pa ulit sa bayan mamaya. Saka pinapasabi pala nung Mrs. Alvarez, barado na naman daw 'yung banyo nila."

"Mga 'to talaga o, kakagaling ko lang sa restaurant kanina, hindi pa pinadala sa 'kin 'yung supply." I shook my head to myself exasperatedly. "Saka 'di ba naayos na ni Mang Sario yung bara kagabi?"

Tony shrugged. "Barado daw ulit eh."

"Uh sabihan mo na lang sila Noy baka luluwas sila mamaya para kunin 'yung supply sa restaurant. Tas hanapin ko na lang si Mang Sario ulit mamaya. Sige, salamat ha," I bade then started out of the kitchen, bringing two plates at a time.

"Uy Topher," Mia started to stand when she saw me come out. "Gusto mo ng tulong?" she offered.

"Hindi, okay lang," I dismissed her, setting the plates down on the table before going back into the kitchen.

Tony had someone else help me bring out the rest of the dishes anyway. On my way back to the table the last time, I guessed I was too distracted or just naturally accident prone, I closed the door over my hand.

"Ow! Shhh—" I cursed under my breath, wringing my hand out from the pain as I glared at the screen door like this was its fault. *This day just kept getting better and better*, I thought, my frown deepening as I walked back to our table, still hissing slightly.

Mia and Leo were laughing, again, still, when I got back and sat down.

"Hindi ko pa siya nakikilala eh," Mia was saying.

"Oo, may article nga about it before," Leo was saying. "He's a tourist attraction in himself. Si Mang Ben." He looked over at me. "'Di ba, pare? Your dad, aside from being famous sa extreme sports, sinasabi nila he speaks better Filipino than most other Filipinos samantalang mas mukha siyang foreigner."

I blinked at him, still slightly frowning. "A oo," I replied.

"Kasi his dad's like half-Russian pero born in the Philippines," Leo explained to Mia for me. "'Di ba 'no, tsong?" he prompted me with a nod.

"Astig yun a," Mia commented. "Sikat pala Dad mo," she said to me. Then she noticed my frown. "What's wrong?"

I shrugged dismissively. "A wala," I said kind of sheepishly, flapping my limp right hand. "Naipit lang sa pinto 'yung kamay ko."

"Aww." She wrinkled her nose, pouting, and unceremoniously took my hand in hers and moved to kiss my fingers. "Kawawa naman," she mumbled in an adorable-little-kid sort of way.

My face flushed red-hot and I just blinked at her, frozen in my seat, my pulse racing. For some reason, I suddenly wanted to move my hand to touch her face but then Leo chuckled, which snapped me to attention. I jerked up straight in my seat and pulled my hand away from Mia self-consciously.

"Ang sweet n'yo naman," Leo commented with a mocking tone of voice, clearly amused.

I shot him a brief dark look before I glanced over at Mia. But she looked just as normally cheerful as usual, going back to eating, and started another topic of conversation with Leo.

I looked down at the food, suddenly losing my appetite, so I just about picked up my fork to start eating when—

"Uy, Kristoper!" Mang Sario called, poking his head into the window of the dining cottage. "Andiyan ka lang pala."

We all looked up.

"Bakit?" I asked, half-standing up from my seat.

"Kanina ka pa hinahanap ni Arnold a," he informed me, waving me out. "Ikaw daw maghahatid nung ibang bisita pabalik sa bayan."

"Ay shh—" I blinked as I suddenly remembered. I was supposed to drive some of the guests back to the city and pass by a few of the sights on the way, like the waterfalls and the crocodile farm. I'd completely forgotten. I looked back at Mia and Leo, still seated at the table, who'd carried on with their chatter and I frowned involuntarily.

Now I had to leave. I had to leave Mia—with Leo, for probably the rest of the day. This was just perfect. I blew out a breath in defeat and stood up. "Uy, uh, kailangan ko na pala umalis," I announced.

Mia looked up. "Huh? Saan ka pupunta?"

"Wala." I rolled my eyes. "Trabaho. Malamang gabi na'ko makakabalik." I started to walk backwards away from the table headed for the door.

"Sige, pare." Leo raised his hand in a wave. "See you later."

I shot him another brief dark look, not attempting to disguise my displeasure at having to leave them alone together. "Ingat kayo," I bid before I turned to go.

"Bye, Topher!" Mia called as I exited the door.

8

Nagseselos ka ba?

I wasn't the greatest tour guide in the world today. Arnold mostly had to cover for me the entire time that I had to show the guests around the tourist spots, since I was irritable and temperamental and grouchy—and for what? I shook my head in disbelief at my irrational behavior. What did it matter if I left them alone? Maybe it was even a good thing, I thought to myself. Mia would find some other guy to fill the role of "psycho girl's boyfriend" and finally get me off the hook. Then I could finally have some time to myself without the whining and irritating questions, being pestered with her usual weirdness.

In fact, Leo would suit her needs perfectly. He was probably making her laugh now, cheering her up, making her forget her problems like what I had planned, except that in *my* plan,

I was supposed to be the one doing that. I was the one who had seen her last night. I was the one who knew. Leo didn't understand. He was just a pinch-hitter with a load of charm and impeccable timing.

I wanted to be there for her, make her laugh. Unfortunately, I was a little slow in the execution. Now it was probably too late.

After I dropped off the last guest at the Hotel Fleuris then passed by the restaurant to get the food supply, we started on the long drive back down to the resort. I frowned again. There was a vaguely nauseating feeling in the pit of my stomach. I shifted in my seat tensely, clearing my throat.

Arnold had been watching me, without comment, ever since we'd left the resort this afternoon. I knew for a fact he thought Mia was great. I actually knew that Mia had charmed practically the entire resort crew—they were all on a first name basis with her—in as short as the two days she'd been there, which actually wasn't surprising because Mia really was great—which was *irrelevant* anyway because I wasn't *really* her boyfriend.

"Nga pala, dadaan daw si Ben sa resort bukas," Arnold spoke up after an hour on the road. "May sasalubungin yatang bisita."

I nodded but didn't say anything.

"Baka may gusto kang sabihin," he quipped.

I knew he was teasing that I should introduce my "girl-friend" to my dad. Normally I would've snapped at him my usual "Hindi ko kaanu-ano yun. May sayad yun." reply but I was too preoccupied thinking about what was going on at the resort right now while I was gone than I was worried about what my dad would think about me in this kind of situation—again. My dad was a pretty cool guy and I was never deprived of things for the most part but of course we had the reputation of the resort to think about. And business was business.

"Matutuwa yun," Arnold said, patting my back in assurance.

I glanced over at him with a slight smile of appreciation. I'd grown up with these people. These people had helped *raise* me. "Bakit?" I asked innocently, trying to dismiss his suspicions with ignorance. "Ano bang meron?"

Arnold reached over and smacked the back of my head lightly. "Ulol, ako pang lolokohin mo," he snapped, good-naturedly.

I couldn't help laughing under my breath.

"Wala namang kaso kung may syota ka na naman eh," he explained.

I rolled my eyes. "Hindi ko syota 'yun. Magkaibigan lang kami," I informed him. "Tinutulungan ko lang siya. Proble-mado eh," I added smoothly.

"Ahhh." He nodded, watching me carefully. "Kaya pala tawa siya nang tawa kanina nung magkasama sila ni Leo."

My grip tightened on the wheel involuntarily.

"Ikaw kasi, ayaw mong patawanin." Arnold looked out the window carelessly. "'Yun, naghanap tuloy ng ibang mapapak-inabangan niya."

I shot him a narrow-eyed look. I knew he was just baiting me, trying to goad me into an argument. It was irritating as hell. It was more irritating to consider that he was actually right. I huffed dismissively. "E 'di mabuti," I said flatly.

"Buti na lang dumating si Leo 'no?" he said. "May iba nang guguluhin si Mia. Wala ka nang problema."

I frowned. *Wala na'kong problema. Lintek na buhay 'to o.*

It was pretty late by the time I parked the van at the resort entrance, past sunset, past dinner. Arnold instructed a few guys to unload the food supply and he let me go ahead into the resort. My stomach was complaining in its own right. I'd gotten a bite to eat earlier when the guests were touring the crocodile farm but not nearly enough for a full meal. I headed to the dining cottage first—and heard laughter.

They were still there. I made a face. Same table. Same seats. Different dishes. Everybody else had gone but they were still there. Jeez.

"Uy." Leo saw me first and nodded in greeting.

Mia turned and beamed at me. "Topher!"

I nodded slightly in return. "Uy, andito pa rin kayo?" I asked, trying to keep the skepticism out of my tone.

Leo chuckled again. "Wala, inabot na kami ng dinner," he explained. "Ang daldal kasi nito ni Mia eh."

"Ako?" Mia asked innocently. "Hindi ako ang kwento nang kwento ha. Ang kulit mo." She laughed.

I looked from one to the other and back, my disposition not improving.

"Mas makulit ka," Leo teased. "Hindi nga ako makatapos ng kwento sa'yo, sumasabat ka na kaagad."

"Hah, hindi naman ako ang umubos ng ulam," Mia said with a mock stubborn look.

Leo laughed. "Eh masarap talaga ang pagkain dito e, 'di ba, pare?" he told me.

"Wow salamat," I replied dully.

Leo blinked, finally noticing my mood. "Uh . . ." He stood up and grinned easily. "Pala, gabi na rin. Mauuna na'ko. May trabaho pa ulit bukas."

"Mm." I nodded shortly again.

"Uh, nga pala, Mia." Leo turned to her. "Sabihin n'yo lang kung kelan n'yo gustong gawin 'yung sinabi ko kanina. May mga kilala ako dun, makakamura tayo."

"Sure, thanks ha." Mia smiled brightly at him.

"Next time ulit, Mia. Sige, pare." He patted my back before he strode out of the cottage.

"Bye!" Mia called, waving at him.

I watched him leave wordlessly.

"Kumain ka na?" Mia asked me brightly as soon as Leo exited the door.

"Hindi," I replied shortly, still in a bad mood, as she on the other hand didn't appear to have missed me at all. Why would she if Leo were here in my place? I guessed it really was irrelevant who was with her.

"Ito dali, tikman mo." Mia waved me over to the seat beside her. "Tinirhan ka namin ng lapu-lapu saka chopsuey saka—um . . ." She scanned the table for leftovers then laughed. "Naubos ko na ata 'yung lechon kawali," she said sheepishly.

I didn't reply. I wasn't actually planning on staying and

eating then and with her there but my stomach insisted so I sat down and helped myself. Mia was still cleaning out the leftover chopsuey on one plate. She was probably so used to my being in a bad mood, she didn't say anything about it and started on another topic.

"Ang kulit pala nu'n ni Leo," Mia relayed. "Kinukwento niya sa 'kin 'yung mga ginagawa n'yo dati, namamangka tapos nanghuhuli ng pusit. Masarap siguro mag-island hopping dito. Oo nga pala, sabi ni Leo, may kilala daw siya na bangkero sa Honda Bay kung gusto raw nating mag-tour. Since kilala niya, baka raw maka-discount tayo or something. Okay yun 'di ba?" she prompted.

The muscles in my neck tensed. Her yapping was irritating me ten times more than usual. I was grinding my food hard, frowning over my plate.

"Saka sabi rin ni Leo may bakery daw sa may bayan baka raw gusto natin puntahan. May branch din daw sila sa Manila. Masarap daw 'yung pianono." She smiled cheerfully. "Alam mo 'yun? 'Yung bread na may sugar? Saka babalik daw sina Leo bukas—"

I swallowed hard, my grip tightening on my fork.

"I-fi-finalize 'yung sinusukat kanina tapos baka raw gusto natin pumunta ulit sa bayan. Na-mention n'ya 'yung restaurant ng Dad mo sa city, baka raw gusto natin mag-dinner or something? Saka sabi rin ni Leo—"

"Utang na loob, hindi ka ba titigil?" I groaned loudly in frustration.

She stopped short, stunned.

I guessed that was a little too harsh. I normally told her off but so far, I had never been able to shut her up.

"Ano bang problema mo?" she demanded with a frown—first actual frown I saw of hers directed at me.

"Wala," I replied gruffly.

"Anong wala? Kanina ka pa iritable diyan e," she pointed out. "Ano? Ba't di ka makasagot?" she prompted.

I met her gaze. I'd never actually seen *her* angry before either. My eyebrows snapped together. But why the hell was she angry? I wasn't the one doing anything wrong. "Ba't ako ang tinatanong mo? Wala naman akong ginawa a," I explained pointedly.

She blinked, her frown deepening. "Ganun? Bakit, at ano naman ang ginawa ko sa'yo?" she asked expectantly.

"Wala," I said again and started to stand. "Antayin mo na lang si Leo. Kayo na lang mag-usap. Tutal mukhang nagkasunduan na naman kayo eh."

"Ha?" She made a face. "Tangina 'to." She muttered in disbelief before she asked, "Nagseselos ka ba?" point-blank.

I gawked at her. "Ha? Hindi 'no," I replied in ridicule. "Ba't ko naman pagseselosan ang ibang boyfriend mo?"

She blinked, surprised. "What?" Her voice raised a few decibels in incredulity. "Are you accusing me of cheating on you?"

I stopped short. "Nooo," I replied matter-of-factly. "'Wag na nga," I dismissed frustratedly and started towards the door. I didn't know why I was acting so territorial. It was just a temporary arrangement. It meant nothing. And it wasn't like I *liked* her or anything. Did I?

"Hoy, bumalik ka nga dito," Mia called with a strange tone, catching up with me before I got out of the door. "Sa tingin mo ba boyfriend ko na rin siya?" she asked, seemingly trying not to laugh in my face.

"Aba, malay ko ba!" I shrugged irritably.

"Para kang gago." She shook her head. "Ilang boyfriends ba sa tingin mo kailangan ko? Ilan ba *dapat*?" she prompted then raised an eyebrow. "Maliban na lang siyempre kung kakaiba ang definition ninyo ng relationship dito sa Palawan."

I was trying to keep glaring at her but her bitten back smile was not to be reckoned with. My anger dissipated. I just rolled my eyes and let out an exasperated sigh at how stupid this whole argument actually was. "Ewan," I said dismissively and walked back towards the table. "Gutom pa'ko."

Mia watched me with mirth in her eyes. "Tangina, nagselos ka nga kanina?" she asked with a short laugh.

"Hindi 'no," I replied defensively.

"'Wag ka na mag-deny," she teased. "Heeey!" she started, going back to her excessively cheery voice as she came over and put her arms around my neck. "We just had our first fight."

I glanced up at her in skepticism and rolled my eyes again. Mia was so incredibly, incredibly insane—and incredibly, incredibly infectious.

9

The Beach

I put away the last of the dishes into the kitchen and came back to the dining area. Looking around, I furrowed my eyebrows when I didn't see Mia anywhere. I blew out a breath and shrugged, guessing she must've gone to her room to hit the sack. She had to be tired from the all-day bonding with Leo, I thought, rolling my eyes as I walked out of the dining cottage.

The sky was clear and the moon shone brightly over the resort like a big spotlight. I was pretty tired as well, having made two trips to and from the city today, but I still wanted to spend more time with her—which sounded stupid even in my head but I dismissed it and started to walk towards her cottage to ask if maybe she wanted to go for a walk or something.

I stopped a few feet from her door. The lights were off. She was already asleep. I sighed, looking around absently, shoving my hands in my pockets and turning around on my heels to walk away. Most of the other guests were already in their cottages, getting ready for bed. Then out of the corner of my eye, I saw someone on the garden path to the beach and looked over, instantly smiling.

"Uy," Mia greeted with a smile when I came out from behind the hedges. She was setting up the chaise lounge, something in her hand that looked like a CD player. I vaguely remember her having had the same thing last night when I'd found her on the beach. "Hindi ka pa ba matutulog?" she asked.

I blinked and shook my head as I walked closer. "Di pa ako inaantok," I explained.

Mia patted the seat beside her on the chaise inviting me to sit down. I smiled again and obliged, leaning back on the chair.

Mia stretched out automatically beside me, my arm behind her head. I glanced down at her still puzzled at how she could feel so comfortable with me when she'd only met me three days ago. And I had been incredibly pig-headed for the past three days too. It was a wonder she wasn't completely pissed off at me when I hadn't been any kind of useful to her as of yet. It wasn't strange for me though. I curved my arm around her to pull her closer. Mia made it so easy to get to know her, to get comfortable with her. She made everything seem so simple.

I breathed deeply, closing my eyes, instantly relaxing, feeling all the stress and tension I had the entire day melt away into the rhythmic crashing of the waves against the shore.

"Ay teka." Mia sat up abruptly.

"Dito ka lang," I snapped, suddenly disoriented as I held her fast, my arm around her waist.

She laughed. "Kukuha lang ako ng towel," she told me pointedly.

I felt a laugh as well. "Uh . . .bilisan mo," I said carelessly and let her go.

"Opo." She mocked with a slight grin, reaching over to mess up my hair playfully before she walked away.

I just chuckled and raked my hair back with my hands. I shook my head to myself in ridicule before I lay back down on the chair, my arms folded behind my head as I looked up at the sky. I shifted in my seat and then frowned, reaching down to pull Mia's CD player out from sticking into my side. I took the earphones and listened to the current track.

Mia returned after a few minutes, towel in tow, and saw me with the player.

I looked up, pressing Pause. "Uy." I nodded. "Anong CD 'to?"

"Okay ba?" she asked, stretching out beside me on the chaise again. "It's a beach compilation," she explained. "Nag-burn ako ng cool sounds para sa beach. Mostly soundtrack ng 50 First Dates, tapos Moby, Ivy, then mostly reggae. Astig 'no?"

I had to agree. Apparently, Mia had excellent taste in music as well.

She spread the towel over us like a blanket then reached up to put my arm around her shoulders again. "The best 'yung re-make ng 311 nung isang kanta ng The Cure," she informed me as she took the player and handed one end of the earphones to me so we could listen together. "Di ba sobrang bagay 'yung mga tugtog sa beach?" she prompted. "As in I listen to this, like, everyday."

"Tumatambay ka ba dito sa beach gabi-gabi?" I asked curiously.

She shrugged. "Minsan . . ."

"Um . . .nga pala . . .kagabi—" I started after a long pause, unsure of how to ask what to ask. I was still working on the presumption that whatever it was didn't really concern me. Only now I didn't care.

Mia let out a light laugh. "A yun, wala yun," she dismissed with a wave of her hand. "Nag-e-emote lang ako. Kalimutan mo na yun."

"Talaga?" I asked slowly, unconvinced. "Para kasing medyo mabigat 'yung iniisip mo eh. Baka . . .gusto mong pag-usapan—"

"Sabing kalimutan na yun eh," Mia snapped.

I furrowed my eyebrows, taken aback. "Ayoko," I countered. "Mia, gusto ko lang naman tumulong—"

She sat up abruptly again, cutting me off. "Alam mo, I don't need this," she said and stood.

"Sandali." I caught her arm.

She whirled around and spoke with an annoyed tone. "Ano ka ba? Sinabing kalimutan na 'yun eh. Hindi ko kailangan ng tulong mo at lalong hindi ko kailangan ang awa mo. Mas mabuti pang wala kang pakialam sa'kin kesa kaawaan mo'ko." She paused, regarding me with a sneer. "Kaya ba mabait ka sa'kin recently?" she prompted expectantly, her hands on her hips. "Alam mo salamat na lang!"

I frowned again, starting to get mad myself. "Gusto ko lang naman malaman kung ano problema mo eh. Bawal ba yun?"

"Hindi mo ako matutulungan," she concluded. "Anyway, I'm not asking for your help."

I made a face, standing up myself. "Not asking for my help," I echoed in ridicule. "Hindi mo kailangan ng tulong ko? Eh ano pala ginagawa ko dito?" I shook my head in disbelief. "Alam mo dati akala ko problemado ka lang, kaya ka ganyan. Ngayon, alam ko na, may sayad ka nga talaga 'no?"

She groaned, rubbing her sinuses. "Look, wala ka namang magagawa maliban sa hinihingi ko sa'yo. I don't want to bother you with details na hindi mo naman aanhin. As if naman may pakialam ka. As if naman friends tayo. Five days lang ang hinihiling ko. Five days na hindi ko ito kailangan isipin, pag-usapan. Mahirap bang intindihin 'yun?" She threw up her hands before she whirled around.

My frown deepened as I watched her walk away. I didn't want to upset her even more. That was the last thing I wanted. But if she was going to be that stubborn— "Pasensya ka!" I called loudly. "Kung gusto mo ng syotang walang pakialam, kay Leo ka na nga lang." I paused before adding, "O baka gusto mo kay Mike na lang ulit."

Stunned, Mia whirled around, scorn in her eyes. "Wow. Alam mo naman pala lahat eh. Ang galing mo," she retorted sarcastically. "Don't talk like you know everything," she told me before continuing to stalk away.

I made a face. Great. I just succeeded into pissing her off

even more. I sighed. "Sa'n ka pupunta?" I called out then. "Dulo na ng resort 'yan," I told her pointedly.

She stopped. "Ano bang pakialam mo?" she yelled stubbornly over her shoulder.

I rolled my eyes. I couldn't believe I had to go through this. One of us had to back down and it wasn't going to be her. I blew out a breath. "'Wag ka masyadong nagsisisigaw," I called, willing to lighten the mood. "Baka magising pa 'yung ibang guests. Sige ka, irereklamo ka ng mga yun."

Mia narrowed her eyes at me and watched me edgily as I slowly walked over to her. "Ginagago mo ba'ko?"

I shrugged, biting back a small smile. "Hey, we're having our second fight." She was still frowning when I peered into her face. "Nakakatakot ka palang magalit," I noted truthfully. "Kaya pala sindak sa'yo sina Ken."

That only managed to dissolve her frown. "Kahit naman kay George sindak si Ken eh," she remarked comically.

I chuckled, raising my hand to tuck her hair behind her ear. "Look, hindi na'ko magtatanong . . .pero sana naman magkaibigan na tayo. Kung kailangan mo ng mapapaglabasan ng sama ng loob . . .or kausap—"

"Ugh. The last thing I want is pag-usapan na naman ito," she groaned exasperatedly. "Pare-pareho lang naman ang kwento eh! May nanloloko at may nagpapaloko." She shrugged, as if in ridicule of herself. "Pero hindi ko lang matanggap. Hindi ko ginustong isiping possible . . . Alam ko na eh—*I should have known*." She threw up her hands. "May iba na pala siyang ka-text, na si Jackie na 'yung lagi niyang kasama. Malaman-laman ko na lang ako na pala 'yung nagmumukhang tanga . . ." she trailed off flatly, shaking her head. "Ang galing 'no?" Then she blew out a breath. "Can we stop talking about this now?" she asked, seemingly tired as she looped her arm around mine to walk us back to the chairs.

My eyebrows furrowed, understanding, and I realized it didn't really matter how it happened. What was important was that I was here for her now. I stopped at that thought and hesitated before speaking, "Mia?"

"Hmm?"

I wrinkled my nose, "Bakit ako ang tinanong mo? Naghanap ka ba muna sa buong Puerto Princesa o sa resort?" I asked. "O . . .nagkataon lang talaga na malas ako?" I followed up with a catch in my tone.

She pursed her lips in thought then replied mischievously. "Malas ka lang talaga," she said, finally grinning.

I shot her a serious look. "Hindi nga. Hindi mo ba naisip na baka masama akong tao?" I prompted. "O baka kung anong gawin ko sa'yo?"

Mia let out a sudden laugh.

I shot her an offended look.

"Ay," she stopped short, biting her lip. Then she made a face and dismissed me with a wave. "Ano ka ba?" She shrugged. "Malay mo ba kung ako pala 'yung delikado. Malay mo mamamatay-tao pala ako." She grinned at a for instance. "Or kikidnapin pala kita." She poked my chest pointedly. "Malay mo balak pa rin kita pa-kidnap, 'di mo lang alam," she threatened, winking at me.

I made a face at her. "Ganun?"

Well." She wrinkled her nose, teasing. "That was until nalaman ko na takot ka pa rin pala sa tuko."

I groaned. "Langya, 'di n'yo ba makakalimutan 'yan?" I complained, turning away. "Sabi ko na nga ba magsama na lang kayo ni Leo eh—"

Mia's laughter rang out into the night. As did mine.

10

Complications

I totally needed a smoke. I puffed out from a new stick, fidgeting anxiously in my seat at the counter the next morning, deep in thought. I hadn't smoked in the past two days—because being around Mia, it was pointless. I couldn't believe she was able to affect my life in such a big way.

"Darating daw Daddy mo bago mag-lunch," Joseph informed me from behind the counter.

I looked up then nodded without comment before returning to my dazed stupor. My dad was coming over today. Like I didn't have enough to worry about.

Joseph shot me a curious look. "Okay ka lang, Chris, pare?" he prompted.

I blinked flustered. "A oo." I nodded shortly again, taking a puff from my cigarette. *Was I okay?* Good question. I blew out the smoke carelessly. I couldn't get the kiss out of my mind. Although, if I stopped to think about it, it didn't even last that long—hell, I didn't even see it coming until it was over. But I was having a hard time sitting still. I really must have been losing it.

Walking along the beach, holding hands, early morning, seemed like a good idea. It was in fact a great idea. I learned that if you made an effort to actually listen to her, Mia's ramblings made a lot of sense and she had an incredible sense of humor—sarcastic and witty. We'd probably talked more in the last three hours than we had for the last three days and I found out that we actually had a couple of things in common. We both hated lollipop mainstream music, liked nature and doing outdoorsy stuff, and we both had a habit of waking up late. With Mia, time was a relative and seemingly nonexistent notion.

In fact, I think we were still laughing about the story that her folks couldn't stop telling at family reunions, this number that Mia had always performed as a kid—couldn't stop to perform as it seemed—and she was coming around behind me, leading my arm over her head in a twirl. The next thing I knew, I was leaning too close to her or she was to me. And the kiss just happened. It seemed perfectly okay at the time. Mia pulled away, smiling as usual, before she went on to tell me about her cousin's baby that was due in a month.

I guessed it shouldn't be anything out of the usual, for a couple I meant. Mia, for damn sure, had acted like nothing strange had happened. So why the hell—couldn't I stop thinking about it?

Because I wanted to kiss her again. I shook my head to clear it and unconsciously put out my cigarette.

Mia suddenly passed by outside the dining cottage, heading to the beach, and I sat up. But she kept walking and didn't see me. I slumped back in my seat, looked in resentment at the ashtray where I'd put out my cigarette then took out another fresh stick and lit it.

"Uy," Joseph spoke up, stopping from wiping the counter, looking outside at something. "Andyan pala ulit 'yung mga nagsusukat nung camping grounds."

"Ha?" I asked, craning my neck to look. *Sina Leo?* I pushed myself off the stool and walked over to the site.

"Uy, pare," Leo greeted me as soon as I came into view. He was supervising a few of the guys crossing the creek towards the other side to finish the measurement of the land or something. There were a few of the resort's crew with them as well assisting.

I nodded in acknowledgment, puffing out smoke, waving it away with my hand.

"Asan si Mia?" he prompted.

I looked at him steadily. "Nasa beach siguro."

"Ay naku, alam mo ba may narinig akong tsismis kanina lang," Leo started with a laugh, patting my back.

I eyed him warily. "Tungkol saan?"

"Tungkol sa'yo," he said. "Natawa nga ako sobra eh. Hindi

raw ikaw ang nanligaw kay Mia tapos under ka raw niya." He laughed then.

Only I think he spoke too loud, a few of the other guys overheard him and laughed themselves. Unfortunately, here in Marlboro Country, men took much pride in their manhood.

Leo watched my reaction. "Bakit, pare, totoo ba yun?" he asked in disbelief then laughed again.

"Magpalaki ka kasi ng katawan, Chris," Noy, one of the resort's maintenance staff, who was assisting Leo's group commented. "Lagi ka tuloy nalolokong lampa. Nakakahiya sa tatay mo."

"Oo nga 'no," Leo realized loudly. "Daredevil ang tatay mo, tapos ikaw—takot pa rin sa tuko."

Everyone laughed again.

I glared at everyone and just shook my head. I was used to the teasing, being as I was, hesitant about taking risks or going into dangerous pursuits. Very un-daredevil-like. I'd heard it all my life. But all I was concerned with at the moment was that Mia wasn't around to hear this. I didn't want Mia to think of me any less than I knew she probably already did. I didn't want to see shame in her eyes when she looked at me. I always wanted to look in her eyes and see what she saw in me. Someone worthy. Not that I assumed I'd passed any stringent criteria but I was here and that was enough.

"Naku, ingatan mo 'yang si Mia," Leo told me, shaking his head. "Mukhang madaling maaagaw sa'yo 'yan."

"Maaagaw ang alin?" Mia suddenly popped up behind me, giving us a questioning look.

"Uy, Mia." I blinked surprised, tossed aside my cigarette then grabbed her hand to get us out of there. "Tara, alis na tayo dito."

"Bakit? Anong meron?" Mia asked curiously, passing me and looking out at the campsite. "Uy, Leo," she greeted.

Leo looked back and grinned at her. "Uy, Mia! Andiyan ka na pala," he greeted. "Ito si Chris o tatakas pa."

"Bakit?" Mia chuckled. "What's going on?"

I glared at Leo pointedly, daring him to tell her what they were really talking about.

Leo met my gaze then just shrugged. "Wala, pinapag-usapan lang namin 'tong si pareng Chris," he explained. "At kung gaano siya kaswerte sa'yo."

Unfortunately, Noy was kind of slow in the head. "Kasi sa sobrang lampa eh baka wala nang ibang pumatol," he decided to contribute so everyone laughed yet again.

I shot him a suffering look and make a mental note to fire him later.

"Wala pang namana sa tatay," Noy added. "Takot pa sa tuko."

"Under pa," Leo tossed in.

Mia laughed and my stomach dropped to the ground. I was about ready to duck and hide then she spoke, "Kayo talaga. Ba't n'yo pinagtitripan 'tong boyfriend ko ha?"

I looked at her amazed then grinned so wide, I thought my face would crack. "Oo nga," I added, putting my arm around her waist. "Inggit lang sila 'no?" I said, giving Leo a smug look before I looked back at Mia proudly. I knew she wasn't really my girlfriend but she was one hell of a person. "Tara na nga." I nudged her to go and half-dragged her out of there.

Mia laughed again as soon as we were out of that area. "Hindi rin naman sila nakakaasar 'no?"

"Eh matagal na yun." I rolled my eyes exasperatedly then shot her a look of relief. "Salamat ha," I said, walking slower.

"Naman 'to." She nudged me. "Para namang papatulan ko sila 'no." Then she added mischievously, "Pero nakakatawa sila ha."

I frowned at her. "Nye, ganun? Salamat ha?" I repeated sarcastically.

"Takot sa tuko," she teased, pulling away from me, laughing again.

"Ang kulit mo a." I feigned offense, pulling her back towards me, my arms locking around her instinctively.

She bit her lip to stop laughing but she was still grinning.

Her mood was catching and I felt myself smiling as well. It was strange how happy she made me feel. I gazed down at her, my heart starting to pound at how close she was to me. Mia's lips curved up slightly as if she read my mind.

I raised my hand to touch her cheek, my eyebrows furrowing at the sudden constriction in my chest as I studied her face. Mia tilted her face towards my touch and I swallowed hard. Then I guessed I was getting a little dizzy, I leaned slightly forward . . .

"Kristoper!" Mang Sario's voice rang out in the air so close I jumped surprised, springing back away from Mia.

"Ha?" I called in reply, looking around flustered.

Mang Sario appeared out from the corner of the dining cottage and his eyes lit up when he saw us. "Andiyan na daw si Mang Ben," he announced.

My pulse raced again. I looked at Mia then looked back at Mang Sario and nodded. "A, okay, papunta na'ko," I told him and Mang Sario went ahead.

Mia was watching me expectantly.

I gave her a wan smile.

"Tara?" she prompted, not reaching for my hand.

I blinked once then nodded in understanding before we walked towards the entrance of the resort.

My dad was already surrounded by the resort's staff, awaiting errands, telling stories, reporting complaints, a lot of stuff going on. He looked up and nodded acknowledgment, having spotted me.

Mia and I walked over. "Dad," I greeted.

"O ano, Chris," He prompted. "Naayos na ba 'yung bara sa banyo nila Mrs. Alvarez?" he asked, glancing over at Mia absently.

I nodded. "Opo, tinignan na ulit ni Mang Sario kahapon," I replied.

"A okay," He nodded.

Momentary pause.

"Ako po si Mia," Mia started on her own, putting out her hand to shake. "Cottage #3," she volunteered.

Dad shook her hand and nodded, smiling. "Ahh, kamusta naman ang cottage #3?" he prompted with a friendly tone.

Mia smiled politely. "Okay naman po."

"O iha, inaalagaan ba kayo ng anak ko?" Dad asked. "Aba eh, baka habang wala ako dito eh walang namamahala ng lugar," he said good-naturedly.

I almost choked out a laugh.

"Ay opo," Mia agreed. "Wala pong problema. Inaasikaso po ni Chris lahat."

It sounded weird to hear her refer to me by my real name instead of her usual "Topher." Mia was proper and reserved, quite unlike her normal unruly self, but just as charming nonetheless. It was amazing how she could be all that and so much more than she seemed.

Dad let out a chuckle. "Mabuti," he said with a nod before walking ahead followed by the rest of his party.

I met Mia's gaze as my dad passed by and she grinned at me again. Mia truly was one in a million.

11

Day Out

We all had lunch together. My dad as usual was like "the force," everything radiated towards and around him. It was like this light went on whenever he was around. The staff all seemed chipper than usual. Dad was a born entertainer, an intrinsic people person. He was great at everything and—he also made a mean adobong kangkong.

I was watching Mia the entire time though. She looked like she was having a great time and she laughed at all of my dad's jokes, even the lame ones. She had nothing but praises for the resort, how efficient, how courteous, how secure—you know, with the whole no-keys notion.

I ate too fast. I couldn't wait for lunch to end. Unfortunately, when everyone finished eating, I was instantly tagged to do some chores, which I couldn't very well pass on, could I?

Leo went back to surveying. Mia went back to the beach. Everyone else went back to work. Or so I presumed. I was working quickly so I could finally have some free time but after I finished all my chores, my dad caught me by the door leading out of the dining cottage.

"Uy, Chris," Dad started. "Sakto. Ikaw na lang ang maghatid kina Mr. Sager pabalik sa bayan."

I couldn't help a frown. "Ha?"

"Idaan mo rin sila sa Iwahig saka sa crocodile farm, 'yung usual," he waved dismissively. "Alam mo naman 'yung ruta. Tas habang nasa bayan ka, ihatid mo 'to sa restaurant." He handed me a brown leather wallet. "Naiwan daw nung isang guest kahapon."

I blinked distractedly. "Uh, okay." I nodded.

"Sige 'nak." He patted my back before turning back into the dining cottage.

Yup. Welcome back, Dad. I exhaled exasperatedly.

I was walking towards the beach to find Mia to tell her I was headed out to the city when I met her coming back.

"Uy, Topher," she greeted me with a smile, toweling off her hair.

It was funny how the names she called me were signs of which mood she was in, what kind of role I was currently to play. I gave her a tired smile. "Uh, kailangan ko raw magpunta ulit sa bayan," I told her with a small frown. I was already looking forward to spending the day with her now that—

"Sama ako?" Mia volunteered.

I met her gaze again. There was an idea. "Um, okay," I said, starting to smile.

"Okay," she chirped. "Bihis lang ako. Twenty minutes."

I watched her walk back towards her cottage, my smile widening. No, Mia never failed to surprise me.

***

Mia chattered on as usual the entire way out to the city proper, only I was talking with her as well for a change. The guests we were chauffeuring were Germans who most probably didn't understand a word we were saying so it didn't matter. Although Mia pointed out the usual stops and certain tourist areas on the way to the city from the resort, relaying in English her tour guide stories about Puerto Princesa.

I didn't get it. That Mike guy had to have been such an incredibly stupid loser to have let her go—which incidentally worked out to my favour because disregarding the occasional insanity, Mia was just amazing.

When we got to the Iwahig Prison souvenir shop, I hopped off the pickup and led the guests and Mia into the shop as per routine before I went back to the park the vehicle properly. I tied a bandanna around my head, under my baseball cap, like I usually did because the temperature at this time of the year was intense. It was the kind of weather when you just wanted to dive into the ocean every day.

I walked towards the shop. Mia was still waiting for me at

the door. She looked up at my head and pouted. "Hey, that looks cool. Gusto ko rin ng ganyan," she announced.

I had to laugh as she took out a handkerchief from her pocket and attempted to tie it around her head herself. I wrinkled my nose at her arduous effort to tie it. "Akin'a nga 'yan," I said coming over to tie it on her head properly, taking more time than necessary as an excuse to be closer to her longer.

She noticed and gave me a knowing look and I let out a sheepish chuckle but she just smiled and wrapped her arms around my waist, looking comfortable.

When I finished, I stuck my cap on her head and nodded in approval of my work.

Mia laughed and pulled me over in front of a glassed cabinet that displayed native items to check out our reflection. "Mukha na ba tayong tayo?" she prompted, making a funny facial expression.

I turned to meet her gaze wordlessly, cracking a small smile. I didn't understand how everything, even the tiniest stupidest things that she did recently, always made me want to just grab her and kiss her. *Damn.* I touched the side of her face, caressing her cheek, and my heart pounded in my chest again. "Mia . . ." I said solemnly in a half-whisper, trailing off. I didn't know what I was going to say.

Her forehead creased in question and she gave me an expectant look.

I dropped my gaze to her mouth and stroked my thumb over it lightly, not thinking.

Mia blinked several times then averted her gaze shyly. I

could've sworn I caught her face flush. "Ikaw ha," she said, pulling slightly away to poke my chest again then gestured around. "Ang dami kayang tao."

"Wala akong pakialam sa kanila," I said under my breath, pulling her back to me and leaning my forehead against hers, my eyelids dropping slowly.

Mia broke a soft smile as I moved my head closer to hers.

"Chris!" someone called.

I stopped short, making a face, and groaned.

Laughing, Mia pulled away from me.

I watched her walk away, down the store aisles to go about looking through the things on sale. *So much for that.* I shrugged in defeat, shaking my head to myself, but grinning nonetheless.

I entertained the German guest who'd called my name to find out what he wanted. Apparently, they wanted to convert the souvenir prices to their own currency. I could've saved them a lot of trouble by just replying "very, very cheap."

Later, at the crocodile farm, after making the tour arrangements for our guests, I directed them to the waiting area while I went to a store to buy some water—for me, since the foreigners had brought their own. Then Mia came up behind me. I stopped in mid-drink. "Mm." I swallowed first. "Hindi ka ba sasama sa tour?" I asked.

Mia made a face. "I'm not really that interested in crocodiles," she confessed.

I offered her the bottled water and she took a sip. "So,

anong gusto mong gawin? Mga isang oras ang tour na 'yan. Kailangan natin silang antayin," I informed her.

Mia suggested we just hang out at one of the shaded waiting areas. "Dapat dinala ko 'yung discman ko," she said when we were seated. "Wala naman kasing 'soundz' 'yung sasakyan mo eh," she noted.

"Sorry ha, liblib na pook lang ang Palawan at iilang istasyon lang sa radyo nakukuha namin," I mocked an apology.

"Pansin ko nga eh," she said good-naturedly.

"Okay nga eh." I shrugged, leaning back in my seat. "Liblib, ibig sabihin konti lang tao, ibig sabihin tahimik. Mas safe. Ewan ko," I said. "Sa'kin lang mas gusto ko sa tahimik. Sa Maynila kasi, parang sobrang gulo."

Mia nodded, already shifting closer, my arm across the back of her shoulders. "So dito mo na balak mag-settle?" she asked, taking another sip of water. "I mean, dito ka na titira permanently."

"Oo." I nodded. "Bakit ikaw?"

"Ako . . ." I felt Mia breathe deeply against me. "Sa tingin ko, masarap magbakasyon dito pero . . .di ako pwede tumira dito." She made a face. "Masyadong tahimik. Parang hindi ko yata kaya 'yung mga lugar na wala masyadong nangyayari. Di tulad sa Manila. Laging may happening. Laking Maynila pa man din ako."

"Ah." I nodded understanding, my eyebrows furrowing at the implications of our preferences. But before I could think more about that, Mia sat up.

"Ay," she said suddenly as if remembering something. "Oo

nga pala. I bought you something." She rummaged in her shoulder bag.

"Ha?" I shot her a curious look. "Bakit?"

"Wala lang. I saw it sa store kanina. I just thought you might like it—" She pulled something out of her bag. "Ay teka, akin 'to," she admitted with a sheepish grin, referring to the colored woven anklet she got.

I chuckled.

"Teka, meron pang ano dito eh—" she said, handing me the anklet. "Pakikabit naman o," she asked, propping her leg over my knee again as she continued to rummage around in her bag.

I obliged, pushing up the leg of her jeans a bit so I could tie the thing around her ankle. But there were already several there—three more to be exact. I frowned and wondered about the other anklets. I imagined they represented other pseudo-boyfriends and I was this new orange one. My stomach felt queasy. I didn't know why I was suddenly feeling possessive.

"'Yun," Mia spoke up later, having pulled something out of her bag again. It was one of those beaded coral necklace things. "This is for you." She handed it to me.

"Uh . . ." I blinked speechless except to say, "Thank you." Again, amazed, at her generosity. I'd never given her anything. She'd said no gifts. Again, not making myself feel any better.

"Isuot mo na," she urged and I obliged. "Okay ba?" she prompted.

I nodded quickly, unable to comment. I didn't care what it looked like. It was from her.

She shot me a look. "Di mo pa nga nakikita eh," she said in ridicule and started to stand.

I pulled her back down beside me, an undefined tightness in my chest, so heavy I found it difficult to breathe. I felt as though "thank you" didn't quite cover what I was feeling at the moment. "Thank you" was incredibly lacking to what I wanted to say. I furrowed my eyebrows, hesitating.

Mia was looking up at me expectantly.

I averted my gaze briefly to get back my bearings then met her gaze again with a slight smile. "Dinner tayo mamaya sa bayan," I suggested. "Sagot ko."

She returned my smile, nodding simply. "Okay."

12

Instead

We dropped the guests off at the Legend Hotel before driving over to our restaurant, Puerto Uno's on Rizal Avenue, to deliver the wallet my dad had me bring and, incidentally, to have dinner.

Mia laughed. "Ang daya," she complained. "Ikaw magbabayad eh hindi mo naman kailangan magbayad dito eh."

I grinned at her. "Well, privilege ko na 'yun," I said as we found a table near the billiards area. "Order ka lang kahit ano gusto mo," I said, handing her a menu. "May idadaan lang ako sa loob."

"Hmm," she said, studying the menu. "Grabe, this looks so familiar." She referred to the menu entries as they were the same dishes we served up at the resort.

I chuckled before I headed into the staff room to deliver

the wallet to one of the restaurant guys. On my way back out, "Uy, Chris!" someone called and I nodded greeting at the group. Some of the guests at the resort and some regulars were here. It came with the territory. Naturally, I had to grease some wheels, make public relations—as quickly as possible. It wasn't good for business to snub guests, no matter how much you wanted to.

It seemed like a whole month before I got through the V.I.P. room and back to the courtyard area where the *al fresco* dining area was. I blew out a breath in relief at having escaped the throng, shaking my head in disbelief and wonder at how my dad did it—and it seemed to come so naturally to him, not to mention it didn't seem to bother him at all.

Now I was as sociable as the next person but it just so happened that I had a date waiting. I started back out towards our table. Mia didn't see me yet. I watched her with a smile. She didn't look the least bit insecure or nervous that I was gone for what seemed like forever. Yup, my girl was all cool.

"Ei." I slid into my seat.

Mia looked up at me with a smile. "Ei," she replied the same.

"Sorry tagal ha," I apologized. "Kung sinu-sino nakita ko eh."

Mia gave me a dry look. "Well, privilege mo na 'yun," she mocked my earlier words.

I gave her a suffering look. "Nye." I dragged my chair closer to hers. "Ano, naka-order ka na ba?"

She nodded. "Yeah, nakita ko nga si Tony eh."

"A ganun ba?" I asked with a frown, wondering why my dad didn't just have Tony bring the wallet and drive the guests down here as well if he was going too anyway. But I dismissed it and looked back at Mia. "So, ano, Miss Garcia?" I gestured around. "Na-tour n'yo na po halos ang buong Puerto Princesa. Ano sa tingin n'yo?" I prompted, as if on an interview.

She considered the question for a moment. "It's okay."

I gave her a mock offended look. "Okay lang?" I asked. "Hindi ba namin na-reach ang expectations mo?"

Mia laughed. "Ano ka ba?" She nudged me. "I love it here. Mas gusto ko pa dito kaysa sa Boracay."

My eyes widened. "Wow," I said, surprised. "Naks naman."

She tilted her head to one side nonchalantly, not looking at me, and I kind of got a sense that something was off. Mia was *quiet*. My eyebows furrowed curiously, reaching over the table for her hand and squeezing it in mine reassuringly.

Mia met my gaze again, gave me a brief smile, before looking around the restaurant in appraisal. "Astig dito 'no?" she commented. "Looks like you've got the corner on the city's night life."

"Yeah, since pansin mo nga before, halos lahat ng ibang lugar dito maaga nagsasara so mga bar na lang tulad namin ang bukas pa kaya dito nagdadagsaan ang mga tao," I explained. "Saka magaling Dad ko sa mga ganyan." I grinned proudly. "Minsan may mga gimik at pa-contest pa silang ino-organize para sa summer. Next week yata may drive-in movie theme silang sine-setup," I informed her. "Astig talaga," I confirmed with a nod.

"Masarap pa food," she attested with a knowing nod.

I had to laugh.

"Your dad's really something, huh?" she started. "Kaya pala he's like a big celebrity around here."

"Oo nga eh," I agreed. "Lagi nga niya kasama sa V.I.P. room sina mayor eh, tumatambay. Sa'n ka ba nakakita ng kainuman mo 'yung mayor saka 'yung chief of police? Dito lang sa probinsya 'yan," I pointed out.

Mia nodded. "Yeah, you won't see that in Manila."

I shook my head. Uh-uh. I leaned back on my chair and stretched my other arm across the back of Mia's.

"Grabe palang pressure sa'yo 'no?" she remarked. "First, you have to live up to the legend that is your dad, tapos you have to be part of his staff, tapos you have to be his son rin." She whistled. "Kaya pala ang lakas ng trip sa'yo ng mga guys sa resort."

I made a face and dismissed it. "Wala 'yun," I said knowingly. "Sanayan lang. Sira lang talaga mga ulo ng mga 'yun. Walang magawa."

She laughed. "Yeah well, I guess everyone's gotta have something to deal with," she said cryptically.

But I didn't notice her somewhat dull tone and weary expression. I was busy playing with her fingers with my free hand. Hers was soft and I lifted it up to my face gingerly, pressing her warm palm against my cheek. I met her questioning gaze after a moment. I didn't think I could explain myself. To say that I just wanted to be as close to her as possible sounded incredibly lame.

"Chris!"

I groaned under my breath again, instantly frowning as I

dropped Mia's hand. I looked over my shoulder, displeasure clearly etched on my face as I caught one of our bartenders waving me over. I nodded shortly in acknowledgment before I looked back at Mia with an exasperated sigh.

Mia let out a short laugh. "Hirap ba ng in demand?" she prompted.

That made me grin, at least, and I winked at her before sliding out of my seat to see what was up at the bar that specifically needed my personal attention.

"'Scuse me," I mumbled, winding my way through the happy hour crowd.

"Uy, pare." The guy in front of me stopped to greet me.

I looked up, looked over at the girl with him then back at him again before his face registered in my brain. "Uy." I blinked at him, "Mike," then looked down at his girlfriend again, giving her a once over.

"Pare, this is Jackie pala, my girlfriend." Mike introduced her to me with a big grin to go with his girlfriend's big teeth and big boo—teeth. "Um." He snapped his fingers in recall then gave me another sheepish grin as if to say he forgot my name.

Typical, I thought, managing not to roll my eyes. "Topher," I spoke clearly.

"Jackie" gave me a sickeningly sweet smile but said nothing.

"Riiight, Topher." Mike nodded slowly, incidentally reminding me of those bobbing-headed-cats-and-dogs for sale on the streets during traffic jam. He looked past my shoulder. "Is Em with you?"

I had no intention of letting him see Mia and vice versa

but didn't want to give him a suspicious look to ask why it was relevant for him to know if Mia was around. Instead, I just nodded shortly and changed the subject. "Kararating n'yo lang ba?"

"No, pare, we were actually just leaving," he told me, his arm around Jackie's shoulders. "This is a nice place," he told me gesturing around. "You come here a lot?"

It took a lot of will power not to boast "Yeah, I own this place." It took a lot of will power not to scuff him. But I managed. "Yeah," I responded then decided to make an exit. Mia might come looking for me and catch up with *us*. "Uh, sige, pare, una na'ko." I gave Jackie a brief smile, "Nice to meet you," before I walked past them, continuing on to the bar. I kept my eye on them though, making sure they were leaving, making sure they didn't happen to pass by our table.

Teng, our bartender, nudged me. "Anong pinapanood mo?" he asked.

I didn't look over at him but dismissed his question quickly, "Wala, pare."

"Chicks ba 'yan ha, chicks?" he prompted with a suggestive grin.

I couldn't help but make a face. *Sure, kung atsay-killer ka,* I thought but didn't say it out loud. Only when I was sure the duo was safely out of our immediate vicinity did I turn back towards Teng to ask what was up.

***

I slid back into the seat next to Mia later, blowing out a breath in relief, hoping I wouldn't have to be called up for duty again. I noticed that Mia had by now made headway on our food that had already been served while I was gone.

She glanced up at me in between spoonfuls of the chopsuey. "Mm," she prompted. "What did you think?"

"Huh?" I asked, confused.

"You think he made the right choice?" Mia asked flatly and continued after a pause. "She's prettier than me, she dresses better, she has better table manners . . ." she trailed off with a skeptical shake of her head.

My expression faded to one of remorse. "Nakita mo sila?" I said rather than asked, since the answer was pretty obvious. She'd probably even spotted them as soon as we'd arrived, which explained her strangely quiet behavior ever since we sat down.

She wrinkled her nose and smacked her palm on her forehead. "Yeahhh well . . . Ehh, it's no big deal," she dismissed. "It's not like I haven't seen them together before or anything. Ang hassle lang talaga sa dinami-dami ng lugar sa mundo na pwedeng magbakasyon, talaga naman . . . Tsk tsk tsk." She shook her head again.

She was obviously not over whatever had happened between them yet. That kinda sucked. I frowned, kind of surprised that she was actually talking to me about this, and kind of unsettled at the fact—now that I really *didn't* want to talk about it.

"Sayaw tayo," I spoke up suddenly, pulling on her hand,

not letting her protest, to lead us to the dancefloor area where only a handful of couples were dancing to a slow song.

Mia didn't say anything. She just put her arms around my neck, her head against the side of mine, and let me lead—for once.

I half-closed my eyes as I stroked her hair. I felt a natural sense of peace and contentment at having Mia close. *Yes*, I thought. Mike had made the right choice but not for the reasons that Mia thought. I didn't know how she could have missed the fact, but she could easily run circles around that Jackie girl any day of the week. Mia was prettier. She was more fun. She was just amazing. And hopefully, notwithstanding the five-day agreement . . .she would maybe also be mine.

13

❦

Action Reaction

Mia seemed more upbeat on the drive back to the resort and I was glad. Maybe I was able to help her after all. Unfortunately, there was more to it than just helping and cheering her up now. Something much more tricky.

"Chris," My dad called as soon as we walked into the resort entrance.

I nodded a greeting at him. "Dad."

He waved me over. "'Lika sandali," he said, not meeting my gaze.

I wondered what was wrong, as he didn't seem to be his usual glowing self. I looked at Mia. "Um, susunod na lang ako sa beach," I said with a smile.

Mia nodded at me then gave my dad a sweeping polite glance as a greeting before she went on her way.

I saw my dad watching Mia walk away before he met my gaze, and instinctively, I knew what he wanted to talk to me about. I managed an instant frown. He didn't even manage to get out a single phrase before I already countered, "Iba 'to, Dad."

He was shaking his head a little. "Nakwento nga ni Arnold," he started. "Alam mo namang hindi kita pipigilan pero gusto ko lang itanong—bago ka ma-develop," he said pointedly, "si Mia, kelan siya aalis?"

I pursed my lips together stubbornly before answering, "Bukas."

He nodded in a big I-knew-it manner. "Gusto ko lang siguraduhin na alam mo 'yang pinapasok mo at na handa ka sa mapapala mo kasi . . .mukhang simula't sapul pa lang eh wala naman talagang balak si Mia na tumagal dito, kahit ano pa mangyari."

My frown dissolved slightly as I knew he was right, as usual. I sighed. "Alam ko," I replied. "Alam ko . . ." I trailed off downcast.

"Hay." Dad sighed too. "Sige, nandyan ka na eh. Ingatan mo na lang sarili mo." And with a nod he let me go.

I nodded in reply then turned and walked slowly towards the beach, deep in thought. It was too late for warnings. *Nandyan ka na eh.* I shook my head to clear it. Mia was here now—with me. That was all that mattered. I walked faster as I neared the beach area, walking straight towards her chair and she looked up, smiling, when she saw me.

"Uy," she greeted.

I didn't waste any time. "Hahalikan kita," I announced.

She blinked at me looking sort of puzzled, but not angry or anything. "Um . . .okay."

It wasn't as though she needed a warning. I just wanted to tell her. I'd been wanting to kiss her again ever since this morning. Everything else just kept getting in the way. I sat down on the side of the chaise, raised my hand to cup the side of her face, and leaned in to kiss her unceremoniously.

Mia didn't protest, didn't move away. She closed her eyes and kissed me back.

It made absolutely no sense. I'd known her for the shortest period of time but she'd managed to infiltrate my life in the most unusual way possible and I couldn't get enough.

My pulse raced a million times out of the normal rate as I deepened the kiss, my hand shifting into her hair and the back of her neck, my chest aching at how much I wanted to say, how much I felt that I couldn't express in words. How being with her had become more than a chore to me, how incredibly special I thought she was and how incredibly lucky I felt, how I wanted her to stay and be with me for as long as humanly possible, how I was almost in love her . . .

I pulled away slightly, breathless, my forehead still wrinkled.

Mia slowly opened her eyes and she smiled as she met my gaze. "Ang sarap," she remarked.

I laughed, pleased with her strange reaction and leaned over to kiss her again, her face cradled between my hands. She was still smiling. *Masarap nga*, I thought and kissed her nose, her forehead.

"Oo nga pala, I forgot to ask. What time ba check-out n'yo?" she asked suddenly.

I stopped short. "Check-out? Bakit?" I asked flustered, still a bit heady from the kissing.

"For tomorrow," she said simply.

Tomorrow . . .tomorrow was her last day here. My heart sank as I was pulled back into reality and I instantly frowned. "Check-out? Uh . . .kahit anong time," I replied, which was actually true. The resort didn't have much for strict rules and stuff.

"Ah, astig." She nodded then.

"Aalis ka na?" I asked slowly.

"Yeah," she replied. "Di ba sabi ko sa'yo, five days lang naman ako dito sa resort," she reminded me.

"Tapos?" I prompted.

She shrugged. "Tapos tapos na," she answered.

I practically heard the thud when my stomach hit the ground at the finality of her tone. It was the same no-nonsense tone I remembered from the first day I met her. She was dead serious. She'd always *been* dead serious about it. I just—I guessed I just thought I could change her mind. "Tapos— babalik ka na sa Maynila?" I asked tentatively.

"Well, I'm meeting my family sa Casa Linda. We're staying there for a few days pa before going back to Manila," she explained.

My eyes lit up. "A few days?" I echoed hopefully. I still had time. We still had time.

"Yeah." She nodded. "They want to do the whole island tour din. Na-inggit siguro," she said with a laugh.

My laughter came out a little forced.

"Owww." Mia made a face, rubbing her arm and trying to get a whack at the beach insects flying about.

I blinked and started to stand, her hand clasped in mine. "Tara, sa loob na lang tayo. Uubusin tayo ng lamok dito sa labas," I said and led us into the screened-in living area so we could sound-trip on the rattan sofa.

The night was quiet so we could hear the waves crashing against the shore from inside. I didn't bother turning on the lights either so the moonlight poured into the windows, illuminating certain areas in the room.

We listened to her CD again and talked for a while about things. Not about Mike. Not about tomorrow being her last day here. But tomorrow when we would go to the Underground River, then for some more touristy sight-seeing in the city, the Honda Bay tour, the butterfly farm—if we had enough time . . .

"I love this song," Mia whispered, snuggling closer to me on the sofa as the 311 remake song played.

Everything was so perfect. *Crap.*

14

The Fifth

I woke up and instantly felt a dread in my stomach. Although, Mia was very much in my arms, her legs propped over my knees, her head on my shoulder as usual as she slept, I couldn't help but feel as though she was far, far away from my reach. I remembered I used to just push her off me. Now I stayed and adjusted my arms around her, pulling her closer, wondering how the hell I got so damn lucky.

I leaned my head against hers, stroking her hair. Lucky *and* unlucky, I sighed in frustration. My heart sank when I remembered what today was. It was the fifth day, our last. Mia was everything I never knew I always wanted—and she was leaving the resort today. She was leaving *my life* today. I didn't want to think about how tomorrow morning would be.

I recalled our discussion yesterday on our living preferences.

According to Mia "masarap magbakasyon dito pero . . .'di ako pwede tumira dito" like any tourist would probably comment. I knew there wasn't anything I could do to change that. This was the way things were.

Mia shifted against me, breathing deeply.

I fidgeted, brushing my hand lightly across her arm. "Mia, gising ka na ba?" I asked in a half-whisper.

"Kanina pa."

I jumped in surprise at her reply as she sounded relatively more awake than I was. I moved to meet her gaze. "Gising ka na pala eh, ba't di ka umiimik?"

Her shoulders shook against my chest with her mirth. "Wala lang," she replied. "Tinatamad pa'kong gumalaw . . . It's too early," she said, stifling a yawn.

I blinked. "Early . . ." I echoed. "Teka, anong oras na ba?" I shifted in my seat to check the wall clock, suddenly remembering we had to leave early if we wanted to do everything we'd planned for today starting with the Underground River. The port for the boats was on the complete opposite side of the island and we had to hurry if we wanted to make serious time.

Mia moaned in protest at my movement. "Maaga pa," she insisted. "Dito muna tayo." She looked up at me, her pout pleading but playful.

I chuckled and resigned, sitting back against the sofa. I had no complaints. I breathed deeply in contentment, stroking her hair as she nestled her head in the hollow of my neck, closer. She nuzzled her nose against my jaw and my entire body warmed. I closed my eyes, trying to absorb the whole sensation of being with her in my head.

With a frown, I wondered how Mia felt, if she even in the least felt the slightest amount of affection back towards me. I wondered if it would matter. If it would change anything. I couldn't seem to accept that we would end this afternoon, just like that. There had to be something more to it, something else. Mia couldn't be that cold, could she? Then again, I really did still hardly know her. I sighed again, discouraged.

"A-hem," somebody cleared his throat from the window and footsteps trudged on the stone path from outside the cottage. Mia and I both jumped and scrambled to a less "awkward" position on the sofa just as my dad pushed open the door and poked his head inside. Arnold was behind him, craning his neck to have a look at us past my dad, and grinning.

Dad rolled his eyes. "Naku, diyan ba kayo natulog?" he asked in disbelief. "Talaga namang mga bata 'to o."

Mia just flashed him a huge grin. "Good morning po!"

I just shot them an uneasy look.

Dad shook his head in ridicule then waved his hand. "May mga sasakyan na papuntang bayan," he informed us, already headed back out. "Bilisan n'yo mag-ayos para makasabay na kayo paluwas habang maaga pa."

"Opo," I replied, slightly embarrassed.

As soon as they had gone again, Mia met my gaze and we both laughed.

"Pasensya ka na ha," I said shrugging sheepishly.

She waved it away. "Okay lang 'yun," she said. "Hindi naman

ako ang sobrang namumula eh." She reached over to pinch my cheek playfully and laughed again. "Para kang guilty," she pointed out. "Wala naman tayong ginagawang masama a."

I smiled half-heartedly, wrinkling my nose and just let her excitedly pull me up by the hand so we could go get ready for our day trip—our *last day* trip. I quickly shook the thought out of my head before I got instantly depressed when the day hadn't even started.

The Underground River was always the highlight of any Palawan visit. Mia was very excited about it. She didn't stop talking the entire more-than-two-hour drive down to the docks, didn't stop talking as we waited for the boat to take us there, didn't stop talking as we waited in line to get on the boats that rowed into the caves.

She hushed only as soon as we got inside the caves and spoke just to point out the several natural sculptures inside the caves that the tour guide showed us. The sculptures, though I had of course seen them before, were really amazing, especially since they weren't man-made. It always made me think that the world had a mind of its own, something we would never have a say about. It was a strange but kind of reassuring feeling.

We finished the tour nearing lunch and made our way back to the boats that would take us back to the mainland. Although there were tables set up in the area for other people who'd brought picnics to the island itself, surrounded by the wildlife, trees and lizards, which were labeled and pretty used to people by now.

"Saan tayo kakain?" Mia asked as we took the path headed

back to the shore, her hand in mine swinging between us as we walked.

I shrugged, watching our step as some of the wooden slats of the path were worn and cracked. "Saan mo gusto?" I asked.

"I think there were restaurants on the other side, sa tabi ng beach, mga kainan," she told me.

I nodded. "A oo, sa Sabang Beach maraming—" I stopped as someone tapped my shoulder from behind and I turned around expectantly.

The man of an elderly couple was handing out his camera to me asking if I could take their picture for them backgrounded by the signboard of the Underground River near the entrance.

"Ay opo, sige po," I agreed good-naturedly with a smile and stepped back to focus the camera. "Smile," I coaxed and the shot went off with a flash.

"Salamat, iho." The man rewarded us both with a warm smile as I returned his camera. Then he asked, "Kayo, gusto n'yo kunan ko kayo ng litrato?" He put out his hand for our camera.

I glanced over at Mia, her camera clutched in her hand. She'd been taking tons of pictures of the views for the past week—only the views, the guys at the resort, not much of her, never of us, certainly none of me. It was like that unwritten rule in her clause: after five days, like nothing, like she didn't meet me at all. There would have to be no proof, especially not pictures.

I didn't want to put Mia on the spot like that. I answered

for her. "Uh, sige lang po, thank you na lang." I nodded politely, backing up.

They didn't insist. They just smiled at us and went back to their sightseeing. I turned back to Mia, reaching for her hand again. "Saan tayo kakain?" I asked expectantly, coming back to our previous topic.

Mia was looking up at me tentatively, I think to gauge if I was upset or anything, but then she looped her arm through mine, our fingers still interlaced, before she shrugged. "Kahit saan."

15

End Game

I stared at the water as it rushed past the speedboat, the motor running so loud behind us, I could hardly hear myself think. Mia could only manage to point out interesting things out in the ocean but not actually start a conversation because of the noise.

"Marami pa palang islands doon," Mia said loudly, near my ear, pointing out to sea. "Siguro mas mura ang mga packages sa mga resorts dun unlike sa Honda Bay."

I nodded.

"Malayu-layo pa ang Dos Palmas from here 'no?" she prompted. "Pati El Nido."

I nodded again. "Kabilang side ng island, sa taas," I explained.

"Underground River naman ang pinakabisitadong feature

sa Palawan 'no? Much more than Honda Bay," she guessed. "Since puro beach lang naman meron sila."

I narrowed my eyes, catching only half of what she said, then nodding anyway as she was probably right.

Mia laughed at our futile attempt to communicate.

"Ang tour na ganito 'pag ipaayos mo sa travel agent mahal masyado," I spoke up, relaying to her loudly. "Mas mura kung ikaw mismo mag-aayos."

"Ano?" I read off Mia's mouth. She still couldn't hear me.

I practically had to yell to be audible over the sound of the motor running. "Sabi ko mahal ang ganitong tour package kung ipa-arrange mo sa travel agent," I shouted again.

Mia was still laughing at my effort to be heard and she mouthed, "What?" still unable to understand.

I made a face at her and couldn't help but laugh myself. I reached over and tucked a windblown strand of her hair back behind her ear, smiling at her. "Sabi ko mahal kita," I said in a normal tone of voice, one she couldn't possibly hear.

"Ha?" she mouthed, furrowing her eyebrows at me and studying my eyes, curiously.

I gave her a mysterious look back before I looked away and looked towards the nearing shore, waving dismissively, "Wala."

When we reached the docks, after a minute, the boatman turned the motor off. I met her expectant gaze again and laughed again. "Sabi ko kung ipa-arrange mo sa travel agent ang package na ganito masyadong mahal," I repeated now that she could hear me.

She rolled her eyes. "Ahh," she said, finally getting it.

I grinned mischievously at her, leaning closer slightly to add, "Mahal na mahal," in a voice just above a whisper and Mia snapped her gaze back to me suspiciously.

I resented the sun for setting.

Joseph picked us up from the bread place up on Santa Monica and was driving us back. We still had the butterfly farm to stop at next, but when I looked down at Mia beside me in the van, her head on my shoulder, her eyes half-closed, I knew the day had to end.

Mia breathed deeply, shifting against me and I tightened my arms around her shoulders.

"Uwi na tayo?" I asked gently.

"Mmm," she murmured.

I smiled to myself, moving to kiss the top of her head before I settled back and looked out the window as we passed the city and the sights so familiar to me. I was so at home here in the province. Everything was laid back, calm, unlike the hustle and bustle of Manila. I entertained the thought of going back to live in Manila for a while.

My life was here. Puerto Princesa was me. Mia was Manila and she was going home soon.

I sighed. *It just wasn't* . . . I sat up slightly, frowning as I saw Joseph turn into a side street off Rizal Avenue which wasn't headed back towards the resort. "Joseph, san tayo pupunta?"

"Sabi ni Mia diretso na daw siya sa Casa Linda ngayong

hapon," Joseph told me. "Kaya pinadala na niya 'yung mga gamit niya, nasa likod ng sasakyan."

I blinked, surprised. "Ah talaga?" I didn't even know she'd already packed all her things. A mix of dread and panic and disappointment stirred inside me as we pulled up in front of Casa Linda.

I nudged Mia awake. "Nandito na tayo," I said with a neutral tone.

"Mm." Mia wrinkled her nose, rubbing her eyes out of sleep and looked around. "Ah," she just said and started to shift across the seat towards the door.

I swallowed, frowning inwardly. She wasn't even going to tell me this was the end of it. She was just—just leaving. I forced myself to accept it and understand. Besides, I had known from the start this was inevitable and it wasn't supposed to be a big deal.

We unloaded the car and I helped Joseph with Mia's bags as she went up to the counter to check in. I remained speechless as I watched her walk back from the counter with the room keys.

"Nandito na pala sila," she informed us, referring to her family who had apparently checked in earlier in the day and were already out seeing the sights. She took the bags as Joseph handed them to her.

"Sige po, Miss Mia." Joseph mocked a salute at her. "Ingat po kayo."

"Salamat po." Mia gave him a bright smile.

Joseph just grinned before he backed away, headed back to the van, to leave me with her.

I blinked. "Nagpaalam ka na ba kina Dad, kina Arnold?" I asked dumbly.

She nodded, still smiling, "Yeah, this morning before we left." Apparently, she'd already said her goodbyes to everyone else in the resort. She'd already planned for everything. "Um, sige." She put out her hand to shake mine.

The scene from five days ago, when she was just asking me to agree to her crazy proposal, flashed back in my mind. She started it. She was ending it.

I shook her hand.

"Thank you ha," Mia said earnestly, holding on to my hand for a while longer than necessary.

I managed a smile. "You're welcome," I replied then withdrew my hand from hers and stepped back.

"Okay." She took up her bags and turned around, heading towards their room.

I watched her walk away for two seconds before I pivoted on my heels and stuck my hands in my pockets heading back towards the van. I hopped inside. "Tara na, Joseph," I said shortly.

"Yes, boss," Joseph replied with a carefully neutral tone as he shifted the van into gear.

Five days down. None to go.

16

Tomorrow

I only got a break from work a few hours after lunch the next day. I automatically headed out to the beach and was trying to relax on one of the chairs. After the five-day commitment with Mia, after five grueling days of boyfriendhood, I was finally able to be alone. The sun was kind of toned down this after-noon and the waves weren't quite so big. It was as if everything was the same as before but a little less.

I shook my head to clear it of depressing thoughts. I barely managed not to think about Mia since this morning because I had chores to do but she was everywhere. She was on the chaise lounge on the beach, inside the living area, inside the dining cottage, under the beach huts, even in the parking lot. I couldn't stop thinking about her and how she wasn't here. I was half-expecting her to pop out from behind the shrubs that lined the beach from the resort and pester me with annoying questions or unceremoniously snatch the cigarette from my hand and put it out. But I knew she wouldn't. She was far, far away in the city and in a few days even farther in a different part of the country.

I sighed heavily, tossing aside my cigarette. I decided it was pointless to try to relax out here so I walked back inside to the dining cottage to maybe get a bite to eat again or get a drink and hang out with the guys or something.

"Uy, pare!" Leo greeted me with a wave. He and the other guys were hanging out at the bar.

Having been spotted, it was too late for me to duck out and leave. I nodded at them as I headed over with a frozen uncertain smile.

Leo slung his arm around my shoulders. "Uy, pare, musta na? Balita ko umalis na si Mia a."

Yeah. Great. Just what I wanted to talk about. I shrugged nonchalantly. "Oo nga," I replied evasively and busied myself opening the can of beer Arnold handed me.

"Ano, nagising ba sa katotohanan?" Noy joked with a snort.

Arnold instantly smacked him in the back of his head to wise him up.

I had to laugh and dismissed it. "Siguro nga," I answered, taking a swig.

Leo seemed concerned. "So paano na 'yun, pare? Tapos na?" he prompted. "Hahayaan mo na lang siya umalis?"

Everyone was watching me, waiting for my answer.

After a moment, Arnold cleared his throat. "Hoy, kayo

diyan, wala ba kayong mga trabaho?" he asked loudly. "Puro kayo tambay. Baka abutan tayo ni Mang Ben dito," he said waving everyone away, himself backing up into the kitchen.

I rolled my eyes knowingly. If my dad caught up with us hanging out at the bar and drinking mid-afternoon, I knew damn well he wouldn't get mad. He probably would have even joined us. But Arnold played his part well.

I swallowed another mouthful before I shrugged. "Ganun eh," I told Leo.

"Sinabi mo ba sa kanya?" Leo asked slowly.

I shot him a strange look. "Ano naman ang gusto mong sabihin ko?"

"Alam ko pumunta silang Honda Bay ngayon," Leo informed me. "Sa'kin nagpaarkila si Mia ng bangka. Ba't di mo puntahan? They'll probably be back like around six or something. Maybe you could ask her to stay," he suggested.

I shook my head. That wasn't gonna happen.

"Huh, sigurado ka ba?" Leo asked. "Well at least linawin mo. Mahirap yang nanghuhula. I mean if I were you, pare . . . Sayang din 'yun," he concluded and just downed his drink.

I blinked and took another gulp. I'd really hate to think Leo was right. Really.

***

"Mia." My eyes lit up as soon as she saw me in the receiving area at Casa Linda's.

Mia's walking slowed and she was looking at me strangely. "Chris . . .what are you doing here?"

I felt a little jolt upon hearing her say my real name and couldn't help a smile. "Um . . .na-miss kita eh," I answered honestly.

She let out a slight laugh. "Ang kulit mo a," she said. "You don't have to do that anymore. We had a deal. Five days is five days," she said authoritatively.

My heart sank again. I wanted to tell her so many things, how I missed having her around, hearing her stories, holding her hand. "May ginagawa ka ba?" I asked, looking over her shoulder to see if maybe someone was waiting for her to finish talking to me.

"Um, wala naman," she replied. "We just got back from Honda Bay. Napagod siguro sila lahat," she explained with another laugh. "Nasa Underground River din pala sila kahapon. Pero 'di natin naabutan kasi we were early," she told me.

I nodded and took a deep breath before I asked, "Um, gusto mong lumabas? Dinner or something?"

"Well, kaka-dinner lang namin eh." She shrugged.

"Ah." I cast my eyes down, trying to think of some other plan.

"Um, you wanna just sit down here and talk?" Mia prompted, gesturing to the native sofa set in the lobby.

I blinked, "O-okay." I nodded and sat down.

She sat on the other seat to my left and I suddenly felt the distance between us unlike it was before. We were now officially just strangers. She gave me an expectant smile, prompting me to spill whatever it was that had brought me all the way here in the first place.

I half-smiled uneasily. It just felt so awkward.

Mia started when it was clear I wouldn't. "So, ano na nangyayari sa resort? Kamusta na Dad mo, sina Mang Arnold, sina Joseph?" she asked.

"Um, okay lang naman," I replied.

She chuckled under her breath. "Asar talo ka pa rin ba?" she prompted with a teasing tone.

I managed a small smile. "Eh lagi naman eh."

She nodded then averted her gaze from mine, seeming to be waiting for me to continue, or maybe trying to think of an excuse to conclude our conversation.

"Um," I spoke up, "saka natapos na pala sina Leo sa pagsukat ng camping grounds."

"A oo." She nodded again as if she already knew this and I wondered if she and Leo were still talking.

I cast a glance at her ankle where she still wore all four colored woven anklets. I should've brought her something.

Mia followed my gaze down to her foot and looked at me strange. "Uh . . .Chris?" she prompted.

"Huh?"

She stifled a short laugh. "Hindi mo ba ako narinig?"

She must've been asking me something when I spaced out. "Uh sorry, ano sinasabi mo?"

"I asked if you had a brochure or something of the resort," Mia repeated slowly. "My sister lost our copy kasi." She rolled her eyes. "Tas my mom wants to check your rates. I've been plugging your resort kasi to them." She grinned mischievously.

"Ah." I nodded. "Well, wala akong dala today eh. Pero alam ko nasa website rin namin siya."

"Oh, you have a website." Mia's eyes lit up. "Which—"

"Oy, Emilia." This teenaged guy emerged from the hall, looking slightly harassed. "Saan mo na naman daw nilagay 'yung camera?" he prompted.

Mia looked over her shoulder. "Sus, asa ibabaw lang ng table eh," she replied.

The guy rolled his eyes before he glanced over, noticed me, and shot me a questioning look.

I sat up alerted and looked over at Mia but she didn't say anything more. She wasn't even looking at me. And the guy just shuffled back headed to their room.

Mia looked back at me again. "My brother," she explained as if in ridicule. "So, your website's got pictures rin of the cottages and everything? Pati 'yung pricelist?" she prompted.

"Um, yeah." I nodded again, only vaguely remembering what the website even looked like.

"Sinong nag-ho-host? Who maintains it?" she asked curiously.

"Uh si Dad kasi ang may alam nung . . ." I trailed off as I looked up and saw the same guy coming back, looking more irritated.

"Huy, ikaw na nga magpunta dun," he barked. "Bakit ba kasi sa'kin hinahanap 'yan eh?" he muttered dismissively, not even waiting for a reply before he stalked back into the hall.

Mia hissed in exasperation then shot me an apologetic look. "Sorry, ang kulit kasi ng mga kapatid ko eh," she explained then started to stand. "I have to go."

I stood up as well, almost in panic as I had nowhere near achieved my purpose for coming over all this way to see her. I was wasting too much time.

"Um, sige ha," she bid with a tight smile. "It was nice to see you again. Ingat ka na lang pabalik." She waved as she walked backwards headed towards their room.

I just watched her walk away, motionless, unsure of what to do, how to stop her, and if I even should. I had to be incredibly thick to let her just walk out of my life again that easily. I swallowed hard. I felt like kicking myself. *Do something.* When she finally turned her back to make her way to the hall, my guts decided to kick in.

"May boyfriend ka na?" I called out loudly on an impulse.

Mia turned around and shot me a look. "Ha?" she asked, looking puzzled.

I watched her expression, suddenly encouraged. "May boyfriend ka na ba?" I repeated as she had to me so few days ago, slightly in dread of the answer I could hardly breathe.

She watched me curiously. "Wala?" she replied slowly with a catch in her tone.

I blew out a breath at once in relief, walking up to her. "Gusto mo magkaroon?" I prompted hopefully, not missing a beat.

A corner of her mouth turned up in an amused smile.

"Ihahanap mo ba ako ng boyfriend o—" She narrowed her eyes to ask.

"Ako," I interjected instantly.

She laughed, shaking her head. "Alam mo, mas sira pa ang ulo mo kesa sa'kin—"

"Mia," I pressed anxiously, easily reading through her trying to change the subject again. I felt like the anticipation and uncertainty were going to kill me. I tilted my head to peer into her face expectantly. "Ano nga?" I raised my eyebrows in question.

Mia stopped then, her smile fading. She met my gaze briefly then looked past my shoulder far, far away, silently as if in deep thought.

I frowned at her having to actually think it over then reached out to tip her chin up with my hand to make her meet my gaze. "Bawal back-out," I stated firmly, earnestly, studying her face.

She pursed her lips before finally looking up again. She met my gaze solemnly, broke a small smile then just said one word, "Game."

17

A Day on Loan

Everyone else, it seemed, was also only too happy to see Mia again. Joseph even promised to cook lunch. My dad wasn't around yet though. I guessed he'd drop by later in the day. I wasn't sure he would approve anyway.

Mia was on an "errand" to pick up a resort brochure, which was of course just incidental to us seeing each other. But because of that, she had to be back in the city after lunch—which gave me quite a tight schedule but I wanted to take whatever time with Mia that I could.

This new temporary arrangement wasn't nearly enough for what I wanted but I decided I would work on that a little later. Right now, I was making up for lost time.

The sun was intense today and it felt good just to hang around the resort. Mia and I went for a swim in the beach, dodging huge waves, splashing water, and kicking sand around. I couldn't remember the last time I'd laughed so much. Mia was different again. She was perky and chatty but she was also thoughtful and not quite so high strung. Mia was all of the above, a little bit of everything, one in a million. I felt a smile as I remembered another thing she was now—my girlfriend.

I watched the waves lap at my feet as I surfaced from the water and walked back to shore. Mia was making something with the white sand. I stood over it, trying to guess what it was.

"Heey! You're dripping all over my Stonehenge!" she complained, swatting me away.

I let out another laugh. "Ah, Stonehenge ba dapat 'yan?" I asked with a mocking tone.

Mia stuck her tongue out up at me, making a face then pointed out to me the several sand structures she'd already made like a castle with a moat around it and the pyramids of Egypt.

"Ah, akala ko Chocolate Hills," I teased.

"Ang yabang mo a." She shot me a suffering look. "Hay naku, Chris, palibhasa wala kang imagination," she countered.

Chris, I flustered, still sort of hadn't gotten over her referring to me by my real name. But I decided I liked it. I dropped down on the sand to sit beside her and sunbathe. "Imagination?" I echoed. "Kailangan ko kasi muna ng inspirasyon," I pointed out. "Em," I tried it out.

Mia shot me a look of displeasure sideways. "'Wag," she said shortly, making a face.

I chuckled at her expression. "Bakit?"

She shrugged, still frowning. "Em's like a whole different somebody," she explained. "I'm not *Em* to you."

"Eh bakit ako?" I prompted questioningly.

She wrinkled her nose adorably. "Weeell, you were always Chris to me," she said after a pause.

I couldn't help a huge grin. Mia made being me sound like it was a good thing.

"But the names—I just thought it would make things easier," she replied logically. "I mean you know how it is for acting, like theater. There's a kind of freedom to be playing someone else." She paused meaningfully. "Besides," she added, smiling up at me. "I like the way you say Mia better."

My grin widened so much I thought my face would crack in half and I leaned closer to her. "Mia," I obliged huskily.

She laughed, the sound tinged with nervousness.

A sudden burst of laughter from the dining area reached our ears. Mia looked over. "Mag-lu-lunch na siguro," she said, starting to stand up.

I held her fast. "Hindi pa," I insisted.

Mia met my gaze. "Chris . . ." she said quietly.

"Wala na tayong oras . . ." I trailed off, almost unrecognizing my own voice.

"'Wag na muna natin pag-usapan 'yan," Mia said evasively, looking away.

I sighed. "Ayoko," I countered.

She shot me a helpless look.

"Bakit ba hindi mo na lang ibigay sa'kin ang number mo—o

address? Pwede kitang puntahan sa Maynila," I suggested. "Pwedeng kitang tawagan araw-araw. Pwedeng—"

Mia was already shaking her head and it kinda ticked me off. It was like she wouldn't even consider it. After everything that I was doing to try and make this work, it was like she didn't even want to think about what happened now.

I stopped short, blew out a breath in a huff frustratedly and stood up. "Bahala ka na nga," I muttered, suddenly not caring, and was going to stalk away when she called me. I stopped walking and glanced over slightly but didn't walk back towards her.

"Chris . . ." Mia started with a sigh. "Ayokong . . .umasa tayong dalawa sa bagay na malamang hindi mangyayari," she explained gently. "It's a big possibility that I never come back here and we'll never see each other again. I just don't . . .want us to—put off our lives because of a few days that incidentally happened this summer."

"Incidentally?" I repeated in protest. This summer was beginning to mean more than the world to me and she was just as easily dismissing it as a mere incident. "Lahat ba sa'yo incidental lang?" I sneered then shook my head in disbelief. "Walang may halaga sa'yo 'no? Kaya pala iniiwan ka," I muttered bitterly.

Mia gave me a highly offended look. "'Wag mong idamay si Mike dito. This doesn't involve him."

"Hah! Wala naman yatang involved dito eh." I glowered at nothing in particular. I knew I wasn't acting very understanding but it wasn't like I was just a third-person observer in this. I just wanted some kind of assurance. I wanted to at least know that this was affecting her as much as it was me.

"Chris," she started after a short pause, sounding calm but firm as she stood. "You understood when I made the deal. I meant for it to end after five days," she said then paused again as if embittered. "Nung nalaman ko 'yung tungkol kay Jackie . . .nagulo bigla ang mundo. I needed—" She shrugged. "To take charge of my life. I needed something that I knew *I* could control," she explained. "Na ako magsisimula . . .at ako naman magtatapos."

My frown deepened. I heard what she was saying but it was as though I couldn't accept it. It just wasn't fair.

"I'm sorry nadamay ka pa but—this wasn't supposed to happen." Mia shook her head.

That frustrated me even more. I whirled around, irate. "Sa tingin mo nasa plano ko 'to?" I asked exasperatedly. "Akala mo ba ginusto kong magkagusto sa'yo? Samantalang alam kong aalis ka naman? Samantalang alam ko na hindi mo naman ako seseryosohin? Sa tingin mo palagay ako nung hindi ko alam ano nangyayari sa'tin? Na natutuwa ako ngayong—"

Mia walked up to me quickly. "I know, I know, I know, I know." She put her arms around me, leaning her head against mine to calm me down.

I tried to even out my breathing but I didn't move to hold her. I didn't expect it to hurt this much this soon, even while she was still here. But obviously, things really didn't often go the way you plan them. I broke off unceremoniously from her and abruptly turned to walk away, headed back to the cottages.

"Chris," Mia called, dropping her hands.

I didn't stop anymore. I felt like my whole world was collapsing and I needed to check back with reality. Mia could make everything seem so simple. I should've known she could make everything incredibly complicated as well. I guessed you couldn't have one without the other.

18

Us. Ours.

Thankfully, the guys gave me things to do. I had to occupy my mind with something else other than things and situations that seemed impossible to remedy. Since Leo's team finished measuring and surveying the site for our camping grounds, we had to clear several patches of weeds and plants that had grown abound in the area. Leo and I were part of the group that had to cross the creek several times to carry wagons, supplies, and some of the refuse across.

It was high noon and the sun was beating down that most of us guys had taken off our shirts to work. I no longer cared about my schedule for today or what I was supposed to be doing. I'd probably already even missed lunch and would have to take it late but I was starting not to mind either. I was feeling pretty hopeless about the whole Mia situation anyway. She was going to leave and I was going to stay. That was it.

Leo and I were taking a water break and I'd poured nearly a bucket of water over my head to cool off. I wasn't as athletic as Leo and was probably going to get a heatstroke real soon.

"Mia!" Leo waved in greeting.

I blinked, surprised as I wasn't expecting her to come around here, and immediately turned my back.

But then she headed over and wrapped her arms around me from behind. "Ang tagal n'yo naman," she said.

I flushed, suddenly inordinately pleased and couldn't resist pulling her even closer, breathing deeply in content. My earlier irritation with her instantly dissipated. "Bakit, miss mo na 'ko?" I asked teasing lightly, as soon my pulse calmed.

"Oo naman," she quipped, squeezing me then after a pause. "Check it out," she noted. "Our third fight."

I couldn't help it. I turned around, put my arms around her and caught her lips in mine. My chest constricted as I kissed her then and there with a note of urgency. Everyone else was probably gawking at us. Leo was shushing over everyone else, yelling at them to mind their own business, and this was most certainly going to reach the genetically large ears of my father but I didn't care.

"Dito ka na lang," I breathed fervently, leaning my forehead against hers. "Mahal na yata kita eh," I whispered, my chest constricting again.

She met my gaze, seeming surprised at my confession

herself. She leaned up and kissed me again. "Mahal na rin yata kita eh," she said softly.

At that my heart pounded and I pulled her closer. "'Yun naman pala eh." I sighed. "Sa tingin mo pakakawalan pa kita ngayon?"

Mia managed a small smile but it didn't quite reach her eyes. "It's not that simple." She shook her head. "Chris, I've already explained this. Hindi ako pwedeng tumira dito. Pero ikaw, this is your home," she said. "I have to go back to Manila tomorrow. This is how it ends."

My frown deepened and I touched her cheek. "Pero paano na tayo?" I asked under my breath.

She moved towards my touch. "Ewan ko." She just shrugged again with a small smile.

I studied her eyes and caught a glimpse of the same pain I was feeling that she was trying to hide in that smile. I remembered the time I saw her *not* crying on the beach. I understood. Mia was an incredibly strong person. And an incredibly insane person. One that I loved.

Mia and I were hanging out at one of the chairs on the beach as usual, my arms around her comfortably, her face in my neck as I ran my fingertips up and down her forearm. Every once in a while I moved to kiss her forehead, trying to stamp the sensation into my brain, but we didn't talk. There wasn't anything left to say to ease the situation anyway. No amount of rationalizing would change anything.

Mia shifted in my arms and I met her gaze as she tilted her head to look at me briefly. "Ang weird siguro," she spoke up, gazing back out into the ocean.

"Ano?" I asked.

"Kung ang una kong nakita si Tony," Mia started, already trying to stifle her laughter.

I laughed myself. "Hm, oo nga." I nodded in agreement. "Siguro masisiraan ng bait 'yun sa kakulitan mo," I commented. "Pero busog ka," I added and that made her laugh.

She nodded then suggested, "Imagine kung si Noy," already laughing harder.

I made a face. "Alam mo ba kung gaano ka-slow 'yung lalaking yun?" I informed her. "Sa sobrang late reaction nu'n sa lahat ng bagay, binibilangan nila yun bago tumawa sa mga joke."

Mia laughed some more. "Ang lait mo!" She poked me in the chest.

"Bakit? Totoo naman a," I admitted innocently.

"Hm . . .paano kung si Leo?" she suggested next.

I blinked, quiet for a while then decided to consider it, thinking how it would be, them together. "Well, hindi slow si Leo," I said truthfully. "Saka pasensiyoso 'yun . . . Matalino pa. Gwaping pa."

"Hm." She nodded slowly.

"Hindi ka susungitan nu'n. Hindi ka aawayin . . ." I continued, sort of remorsefully, remembering the many times I'd pissed her off and been nothing but irritable. "Lagi kang papatawanin," I added. "Gagawin lahat ng gusto mo."

She nodded again in silent agreement.

I had said before Leo would have been perfect for her short-term needs. He'd provide her with everything she needed and more, then just plainly stop when the expiration date hit. Unlike with me, giving her all this hassle even after the contract was supposed to be long over. "Wala kang problema kay Leo," I pointed out.

"Wala nga," she said softly.

My chest constricted again. I guessed she was majorly rethinking her selection criteria and regretting that I was the first moron she'd asked.

But then she shifted closer to me again, sighing. "Hindi siguro ganito kahirap iwan si Leo," she whispered.

I swallowed hard, my chest starting to heave, my frown deepening and I leaned down and kissed her again with everything I felt. Mia kissed me back with the same. No matter what happened next, this summer would be anything *but* incidental. We didn't have to keep up a probably hopeless long-distance relationship, wouldn't have to try to keep in touch, wouldn't have to worry, wouldn't have to doubt . . . because we already knew . . .

19

Today

I sat on one of the chaise lounges on the beach, my face in my hands as I leaned with my elbows propped on my knees, listening to Mia's CD playing on the portable stereo on the sand. Until the end, she was still giving me things.

The package had been left for me at the front desk at Casa Linda this morning. No note. No nothing else. Typical, I shook my head dejectedly. Then again this was probably all *my* fault. If only I hadn't taken her that seriously, this wouldn't have happened. Things would've been better off if I'd kept believing that she was simply nuts. No, no, this was all Mike's fault. If he hadn't shown up at Ka Lui's that night, I wouldn't have thought Mia *wasn't* nuts and this wouldn't have happened. Or it was Mia's fault, being all amazing and inordinately likeable and really kind of nuts in an adorable kind of way.

I shook my head again. There *was* no one to blame.

"Uy," my dad greeted as he walked over from behind the hedges coming from the resort. He sat down next to me on the chaise.

I nodded a wordless greeting, not moving any more except to flick away my cigarette.

Dad just sighed to himself, looking out into the ocean, not saying anything—which was well enough. I didn't really need to hear the words I-told-you-so because *I* told me so. Only, there were some things you told yourself but didn't necessarily follow either way, no matter how right you knew you were.

Mia had come and gone from my life. That was it. All the choices and decisions I'd made in the past week were now irrelevant. But I wasn't angry anymore. I was glad to have known her even for the little while, to have had that kind of happiness for a time, to have experienced and shared a special week with her. I was glad because that was the only thing I could really be.

I was sure Mia had her reasons for leaving the way she had. I guessed it was all for the best. I frowned as the sound of her laughter rang faintly in my mind. I missed her. I missed her already. With every setting of the sun, with every drive down to the city, with every trip to every tourist spot—Mia would be as local to me as Puerto Princesa.

Maybe someday. . .

"Alam mo, 'nak," Dad started to speak. "Ang mga turista dito, para lang 'yang alon sa dagat. Dumadaan lang, hindi nagtatagal. Dadalaw sa bawat dalampasigan, tapos aalis, malayo ang nararating—"

"Pero bumabalik naman sila, 'di ba?" I asked quietly, staring out into the horizon.

I heard him breathe deeply as he sat up, squaring his shoulders, then he patted my back consolingly. I looked up and met my dad's gaze. And he nodded.

I sighed heavily, turning my gaze back out to the orange sun as it set over the ocean and the last strains of 311 mingled with the wind.

The End.

"It is a truth universally acknowledged, that a single man in possession of a good fortune must be in want of a wife." But what if Mr. Darcy was Filipino?

A rich, new neighbor has moved into the house across the street from Armi Benitez and her decidedly middle-class family. The male heir of the house falls in love with Armi's elder sister. Meanwhile, Armi cannot stand his also-rich-assin, arrogant best friend named Will Salcedo.

Parties, dancing, betrayal, intrigue. A Jane Austen classic romance in the 21st century setting of South Manila, Philippines.

Even if you've never read Jane Austen's classic novel, if you love enemies-to-lovers, clean & wholesome love stories, you'll enjoy this adaptation of this timeless romance.

About the Author

ZARA IRIGO hails from Las Pinas City, Metro Manila. She grew up in the nineties when everything was just a shade better. She writes contemporary and fantasy fiction in her default language – Taglish.

Her first book, a contemporary chick lit romance "Five Days in Palawan" was published in 2007. Her modern-day Filipino retelling of the Jane Austen classic romance "Pride and Prejudice" entitled "So Yabang" is OUT NOW!

Sign up to her mailing list to hear about book news first.
https://bit.ly/keepintouchwithzara

Follow her on Facebook
www.facebook.com/fivedaysinpalawan

Follow her on Instagram
www.instagram.com/fivedaysinpalawan

Other Books by Zara Irigo

Okay, Life.

Set in the early 2000's - the days before social networking, the era of the mallrats, when people still used pay phones and landlines, texting was only on the rise, and NU 107 was still on the air.

Lia Alvarez, an 18-year old student, takes up 'the antipatiko challenge' when her fate collides (literally) with Jeffrey Gutierrez, the hottest guy ever with a hidden backstory.

A love story, but mostly a life story. A tribute - to the 90's kids. *This book is FREE for mailing list subscribers.*

Ghosts of Unfinished Stories Past

What if nahanap mo na yung soulmate mo? Pero fictional character pala siya. What's more, ikaw pala ang nag-imbento sa kanya. Sa dinami-dami ng kwentong nasulat mo, sa dinami-dami ng mundong na-imbento mo, saan kayo magtatagpo? Magkakatuluyan ba kayo sa wakas?

Lea Ignacio takes the phrase "getting lost in your books" to a whole new level. Then again, as the saying goes, reading is an escape from reality. But what if...you couldn't escape from your escape...? *Coming Soon.*